SCORPIO

Book 6

Dragon's Claw

ALEX McDONOUGH

iBooks
Habent Sua Fata Libelli

iBooks
Manhanset House
Shelter Island Hts., New York 11965-0342

bricktower@aol.com • www.ibooksinc.com

Library of Congress Cataloging-in-Publication Data
McDonough, Alex.
Scorpio Dragon's Claw
p. cm.

1. Fiction—Science Fiction—Time Travel.
2. Fiction—Science Fiction—Alien Contact.
3. Fiction—Romance—Time Travel.
Fiction, I. Title.

978-1-59687-673-6, Trade Paper

Developed by Byron Preiss
Editor: John Betancourt
Cover Painting by Kevin Johnson
Special thanks to Janet Fox

January 2024

SCORPIO

Book 6

Dragon's Claw

ALEX McDONOUGH

Books in the *Scorpio Series*

Scorpio

Scorpio Rising

Scorpio Descending

Scorpio Dragon's Blood

Scorpio Dragon's Eye

Scorpio Dragon's Claw

GALACTIC OVERLORDS

The vVos lumbered out onto the balcony, followed by two of Scorpio's bodyguards. "There, look there," it said, gesturing with one long hairy arm toward an exceptionally bright point of light.

"I believe," said Scorpio, "that's the Hunters' home planet."

"Exactly," said the vVos.

As Scorpio watched, not knowing what to expect, there came a slow brightening of the light from Hunters' world. Suddenly a spear of radiance shot out from it. When it was over, all that remained was a vague smudge that looked like smoke. It took Scorpio several minutes to realize what he had just seen—the destruction of a world.

"It was necessary to show our disapproval," said the vVos. "The Hunters failed to fulfill their bargain. We hope you are more sensible."

Table of Contents

Chapter One

Scorpio slipped in through the metal doors while his bodyguards kept the cheering crowd back. As the doors slid closed automatically and bolted themselves with a loud clack, he leaned against a wall and sighed.

"Are you okay?" asked Gron, one of Scorpio's guards, his voice low and deferential.

"They love me so much, they nearly trampled me to death," said Scorpio, wiping sweat from his brow.

"They can't help getting excited when the Great Liberator appears among them," Gron explained. Scorpio noticed that Gron's expression indicated disappointment in finding out that his Liberator was only an everyday Aquay like himself—same thick gray skin, beaklike mouth and large blue-green eyes.

"I'm sorry," Scorpio said, unable to escape the feeling that he was apologizing for being simply another mortal creature and not the god Gron had expected to find. "I don't mean to seem angry. I love my people. I spent centuries traveling through time in the attempt to free them from their oppressors."

Gron's look of surprise made Scorpio rephrase. "My orb," he said, patting his belt pouch where the time-travel device rested. "The orb allowed me to travel through time, helping to create my own heroic legend."

"Oh, yes, everyone has heard of the orb that gives you your powers," said Gron, nodding fiercely. Scorpio saw that he was only confusing his bodyguard with talk of creating legends. Sometimes he had trouble following it himself.

The below-ground corridors of Chanamek, the former enemy capital, were dim and silent. The stout doors shut out all sounds of the crowd's cheering and shouting. Scorpio found it comfortingly ironic that he had set up his Liberation Headquarters in the Hunters' stronghold.

Gron walked alongside Scorpio as he moved off along a metal-walled corridor, while the other two guarded the door. It was more of a courtesy than a necessity, Scorpio knew, because their enemies the Hunters were no longer a threat. The small remnant who had survived the fighting was allowed to return to Hunters' World. Scorpio didn't think they would be back.

However, the Hunter occupation had left Terrapin in shambles. Leadership was vitiated from ages of slavery; the economy had to be rebuilt. When he dreamed of freeing his people, Scorpio's thoughts hadn't gone beyond triumphantly routing the Hunters. He hadn't thought about afterward.

This was afterward, and the responsibility often weighed heavily upon him. He sometimes wished for just a blue expanse of water under a sunlit sky. He would dive deep and—

"Uh, what is that, sir?" Gron was indicating a series of towerlike metal constructions surrounded by a metallic webwork.

The corridors were filled with remnants of the Hunters' technology, but this one made Scorpio stare. "I didn't realize that these had survived," he said. "I ordered them dismantled right after the Hunters were defeated and the last few fled to their own world. Or at least I think I did."

"What, what is it?"

"I'll show you," said Scorpio. He stepped into a cage-like device and invited Gron to join him. The bodyguard did so. Gron gasped in surprise as Scorpio pushed a button and made the elevator rise. The old device groaned and swayed as it rose, but otherwise seemed sound enough. When it had reached the cargo-bay doors, Scorpio touched another button and the doors hissed open.

The cargo hold was filled with tier upon tier of tanks, now empty, their transparent sides cloudy with grime. Scorpio's imagination filled the tanks with swimming occupants: fry, the water-breathing children of the Aquay race.

"I don't understand," said Gron. "What was this for?"

"Each of those tanks held one or more Aquay fry. The Hunters were raising them for shipment to another world. As if they were only so much cargo."

"But where were they to go? What was to happen to them?"

"The ships were programmed for a destination, but we couldn't figure out where it was. The Hunters could only say the fry were destined to be an offering to their gods, the vVos. Obviously, they were confused. Gods don't need to eat."

Gron shuddered. "I see why you ordered the other ships dismantled. This is a terrible thing. We must have these ships eliminated at once."

Scorpio stepped back into the elevator. Gron joined him and the device began to descend jerkily. "No, I see I was mistaken to try to get rid of the ships," said Scorpio. "It's all too easy for us to forget once these reminders are gone. To forget and become complacent."

"We could make it sort of a museum," said Gron, "with a plaque telling the story you just told me."

Scorpio nodded distractedly. It was hard for him to shake off a feeling of foreboding that had come upon him in the abandoned ship. If the vVos really existed somewhere, he wondered what reaction they would have toward waiting for a cargo that never arrived.

Gron left Scorpio at the entrance to his suite of offices. As Scorpio entered, a harried-looking secretary rushed up to him. “We’ve been looking for you everywhere,” he said. “The meeting has already begun.”

“Meeting?” Scorpio drew a blank. It seemed his life was filled with meetings and conferences these days.

“You know, the one about land redistribution. You were late so Leah decided to start without you, though I told her that little could be done without the Liberator.”

As Scorpio entered the conference room, the babble of voices died. He saw Leah standing at the podium. She had been his companion throughout his adventures, ever since he had met her in fourteenth-century Avignon, on a planet called Earth. They had become friends, even sharing each other’s thoughts through use of the time-traveling orb, so her appearance shouldn’t have been startling. Still, he couldn’t help noticing the contrast between her pale skin and full head of dark hair, and the hairless gray skins of the Aquay who were gathered there.

“It’s about time,” she said disgustedly as he walked in, though everyone else in the room continued to stare at Scorpio in an awed manner. The Aquay all remained silent, as if waiting for him to make some pronouncement.

“I forgot,” said Scorpio. “And besides, I was having trouble escaping the crowds.”

“Oh, yes, the crowds,” said Leah wryly. “Come up here and let’s get started. I’m sure we can come to some agreement now that *you’re* here.”

The meeting did go smoothly once Scorpio was there, but Scorpio wasn’t sure that made Leah any happier. He had to admit she had worked as hard as anyone in rebuilding Terrapin, but she was often brusque, sometimes even angry.

He wondered if she might be jealous since he had received so much recognition for his efforts. She had received almost none because her part of the plan had been carried out behind the scenes.

Well, it's not my fault the people love me, he thought with a sigh as the discussion continued.

• • •

When the conference had ended, and the participants had gone out, Scorpio looked at Leah. "I think that went very well," he said.

She only gathered her papers and then walked away, without looking back. Scorpio followed her as she stalked toward her own office. "What's the hurry? This was the last meeting scheduled for the day."

"Listen to him talk of schedules," said Leah. "As if he knew meetings were held at a certain time so that everyone could benefit."

"I don't see what the problem was," said Scorpio. "I wasn't very late, and everyone was most accommodating when I did get there. Unless *that's* the problem."

"You think I'm jealous . . . of you?"

"It wouldn't be so surprising," said Scorpio. "The Aquay mob me every time I appear in public. My story is played and replayed on watervision, but you're hardly mentioned—even though you worked as hard as I did, put yourself in as much danger, and all for a race that isn't your own."

"I'm partly the reason for your status as a hero," said Leah, "but I couldn't have known that I was creating a golem."

"Maybe I have changed since you first met me," said Scorpio, "but do you really consider me such a monster?"

"I don't blame you for it. No one could have so much attention paid him and not be affected by it. But no, I'm not jealous of your fame. And I want to keep working for your people, until they're ready to govern themselves again. It's just that I've been feeling homesick."

"Oh." Scorpio felt embarrassed; he hadn't understood the problem. Of course, since they hadn't been using the orb much, their telepathy had faded. Maybe she was right and he had changed—perhaps not for the better. It was difficult to be a Great Liberator and retain some measure of humility.

By this time they had reached Leah's office. She opened the door and ushered him inside. "I'm glad you brought this up," she said. "I've been meaning to talk to you about it, but things have been so hectic."

"I can understand how you miss your home-world," said Scorpio, "but I don't see how you can leave now. I don't know what I'd do without you." He was surprised to hear the pleading note in his voice. Leah had been with him through his worst moments. Even though she was an alien, she was his best friend.

"That's what I thought, too," said Leah, "and then I remembered, time isn't a problem for us."

"The orb," said Scorpio.

Leah went to a small safe and opened it. A golden radiance spilled out into the room. Leah brought forth an orb identical to Scorpio's own. "When the Hunter Prime was killed, in the confusion I picked up her orb. I put it here for safekeeping."

"Now each of us has an orb," said Scorpio. He took his own orb from its pouch and set it on the desktop beside Leah's. Both spheres glowed comfortingly like twin lamps.

"Not that this does me any particular good," said Leah with a wry smile. "You're the only one except for the Hunters who has mastered their use. This is my plan. You teach me to use the orb and then I can return to Earth. I stay there as long as I like and then I return here a few minutes after I left. I know the orb keeps its passenger from being in a situation where he might meet himself, but if I go from world to world, it shouldn't be a problem."

"It sounds a little complicated, but would probably be workable. Do you know where and when you'll go on Earth?"

"Not really. I know I'm not going back to fourteenth-century Avignon. I never really fit in there anyway, and there are too many bad memories. But there must be lots of other good possibilities. With the orb I can sample them all. Why not?"

"Why not," said Scorpio, though the thought of her leaving made him uneasy. He supposed it was selfish of him to want her to stay, but that was what he did want. "I'll be glad to teach you to use the device. We can begin tomorrow. This time I'll pay close attention to my schedule."

Leah laughed. As she bent to place the orb back in the safe, it began to coruscate, throwing a prismatic show of colored lights against the wall. The door of the safe cut short the display.

Scorpio and Leah grew close once again as he taught her how to use the orb, though that wasn't too surprising, since their minds had become synchronized as they moved through orb space. Seeing himself through her eyes, Scorpio realized that he had become more pompous and self-serving. He had let himself be carried away by the people's enthusiasm for a hero; he had believed his own publicity, as Leah would have put it. Though he was aware of Leah's plan to return, Scorpio felt sad as she readied herself to leave for Earth.

"You're sure you have the coordinates memorized?" Scorpio asked. "This can be a little tricky. You remember how I floundered about through time when I first got the orb."

"I'll be fine," said Leah. "You taught me well. I won't say goodbye because I'll be back in a few minutes."

Scorpio enfolded her in an awkward hug anyway, then stepped back as a golden orb bubble began to form around her. Leah's image faded as the bubble dissolved.

Chapter Two

Scorpio was still watching her disappear as the door hushed inward and the secretary appeared, looking even more harried than Scorpio had ever seen him look. The Aquay's eyes were fairly popping, though they were protuberant to begin with.

"Don't interrupt me now," said Scorpio. "I'm waiting for Leah to come back from Earth."

"But, sir, you need to know that an ambassador has arrived."

Scorpio turned toward the secretary in confusion. "An ambassador? Ambassador from where?"

"He says he represents the vVos. He says he has some questions about a shipment."

Scorpio looked regretfully at the space Leah had just vacated. "We must set up a meeting," said Scorpio. "He breathes our air?"

"I assume so; he didn't seem to be suffocating when I saw him."

"Then I suppose we can meet in the main Council Chamber. Set it up. I'll be along shortly."

Scorpio didn't feel the bravado he had shown before the secretary. The feeling of foreboding that had haunted him on the ship had returned. Not only did he have to face the unknown, he had to face it without Leah.

He returned to his own quarters and put on his sea-green cloak. It wouldn't hurt to look the part of the Great Liberator, even though he didn't feel like one at the moment. On his way to the Council Chamber, he picked up Gron and two other bodyguards. Since he didn't know anything about the vVos, their idea of a conference might include violence. Any being who could terrify the fierce Hunters was worth respecting.

When he could delay no longer, he set out for the Council Chamber. He found the room almost empty except for a single being sitting in one of the high-backed chairs. Scorpio was surprised the ambassador didn't have an entourage, but a little reassured, too. A single vVos probably meant they really intended to talk, not make war.

Though it was seated, the creature looked about the same height as Scorpio but twice as wide. Coarse brown hair covered both its head and its body, obviating the need for clothing. The head was quite small, a tiny knob atop huge shoulders and a proboscis jutted from the fur where a face should be, though no other features were visible. To Scorpio the vVos looked more like an animal than a sentient creature, though he noticed that its dark-skinned six-fingered hands were delicate-looking.

With a flourish of his handsome cloak, Scorpio entered the room and seated himself across the table from the vVos. His guards followed and stood to either side.

"Welcome to Terrapin," he said. "I am Scorpio, sometimes known as Raniki the Liberator."

"We are the vVos of the planet Tamir," said the creature. It took Scorpio a moment to understand the words, since they were low-pitched and garbled. It was as if its voice burbled up out of a swamp. The thing had a very small mouth and,

Scorpio supposed, only a crude vocal apparatus. He didn't miss the fact that it spoke the language of the Aquay, no matter how badly it was rendered.

"We have been waiting for the promised shipment from this world. A thousand swimmers, physically active and in the best of health. As agreed."

Scorpio wasn't sure how to begin. "The agreement was not between your race and mine, but between yourselves and the Hunters. I suggest you take it up with the government on Hunters' World, if you can still find any government."

"The Hunters are of little importance to us now that they have proved themselves so weak, but when the vVos strike a bargain we are accustomed to having things carried out according to our wishes."

"Perhaps you don't understand," said Scorpio. "These 'swimmers' you are asking for are the children of our race. The Aquay go through a water-living stage and metamorphose into land dwellers. The vVos are a sentient race. You would surely not want to take away our children, or to, er, utilize them as food."

"One thousand live swimmers, all in the best of health," insisted the vVos. "Shipment to be made within three of your days. I'm sure you will cooperate."

Scorpio felt as if he were arguing with a machine, so easily did the vVos put aside the considerations of family love and posterity. He wondered what sort of society this creature came from.

"All right, try to imagine this," said Scorpio. "The Aquay have no intention of keeping this ridiculous bargain. It was none of our doing in the first place. You will return to your own world, giving thanks that the word has not yet spread about the child-eaters. If it had, mobs of Aquay would tear you into tiny bits." Scorpio made rending motions with his hands, but the vVos remained seated calmly.

"It is all the same to us if you want to be difficult. We will need some sort of accommodations, some sustenance for the body. Fruit is acceptable."

"You're inviting yourself to stay?"

"Only for a few hours. We will have something to show you after the sun sets."

Scorpio made a noise of disgust. "Gron, arrange for a sleeping room and something for the ambassador to eat. You're certainly brave to accept our hospitality under the circumstances. Do you want someone to taste your food before you dine?"

"You cannot kill us that way," said the vVos, and though it was hard to tell, Scorpio thought he heard a hint of amusement in the deep, garbled voice.

The vVos rose and shuffled out after Gron.

"What's that?" a familiar voice asked.

Scorpio looked up. "Leah, you're back!"

"I said I would be, but I was a little disappointed to come back to an empty room. Couldn't you have waited the few minutes that I was gone?"

Scorpio explained the situation with the vVosian ambassador. He thought Leah looked, in some inexplicable way, older, though it was more in her expression than anything else. "Anyway, I'm glad you got back," he said. "We're in a crisis here."

"So I see."

"But I didn't ask you about your trip to Earth."

"I'd really rather not talk about it," said Leah. "One crisis at a time. Did you tell Gron to post a guard at the vVos's door? If the Aquay find out he's here anything could happen. It sounds as if we need to keep him alive—at least until after sunset—so we can find out what he has on his mind. That is, if so small a head has room for a mind."

"I'll send word to Gron at once to have him guarded. He's not a beauty, is he?" said Scorpio. "My first thought was that he was some kind of animal."

"I think we'd better not underestimate the vVos," said Leah. "Maybe we should try to find out more about him."

"How?"

"Well, how did he get here? If he has a ship, where did he land? Is he really alone, or does he have an army in hiding?"

"I won't pry into what happened on Earth," said Scorpio, "but I'm glad you came back. We *need* you, Leah."

• • •

Hours later Scorpio and Leah stood on a small balcony on one of Chanamek's tallest buildings. Terrapin's green-gold twilight was fast fading, submerging detail of the streets below into shadow. Streetlights were beginning to come on.

"Well, we're here," said Scorpio, "but where is the ambassador?"

"No doubt he means to heighten the suspense," said Leah, "for whatever performance he has in mind. My spies came back without much of substance to report. They could find no ship or landing place. The first Aquay to see him claimed he appeared out of nowhere on a public street."

Scorpio put his hand up for silence. They heard a sound—the whisper of pneumatic doors opening. The vVos lumbered out onto the balcony, followed by two of Scorpio's bodyguards.

"Ambassador, this is Leah de Bernay, my second-in-command. She was instrumental in the liberation of the Aquay."

The vVos spared her a single glance, then as if dismissing her, lurched to the balcony's edge and scanned the rapidly darkening expanse of night sky. A few stars had appeared.

"There, look there," muttered the vVos, gesturing with one long hairy arm toward an exceptionally bright point of light with a reddish hue.

"I believe," said Scorpio, "that's the Hunters' home planet."

"Exactly," said the vVos.

As they watched, not knowing what to expect, there came a slow brightening of the light from Hunters' World. Suddenly a spear of radiance shot out from it. At this distance it looked like a mere flicker of light against that vast background of darkness. When it was over, all that remained was a vague smudge that looked like smoke. The planet no longer shone in that sector of sky. It took Scorpio several minutes to realize what he had just seen—the destruction of a world.

"You destroyed them all," Scorpio said.

It was not that he had that much empathy for the Hunters after their conflict. It was simply that his mind was numbed by the concept. He tried to envision what must have happened—the earth trembling, Hunters running and screaming, trying to escape the destruction. His imagination just wasn't up to it.

"No, it's an illusion of some kind," said Leah, betraying that she wasn't doing any better than Scorpio at accepting what was before her eyes.

"It's too far away for a truly spectacular demonstration," said the vVos. The polysyllabic words came out incredibly garbled. "But it should give you an idea of our capabilities."

"He's trying to trick us," Leah said.

"As incredible as it seems, I think he was responsible for what we just saw," said Scorpio. "No wonder the Hunters considered the vVos to be gods."

"It was also necessary to show our disapproval of those who proved unworthy," said the vVos. "The Hunters failed to fulfill their bargain. We hope the Aquay are more sensible. One thousand swimmers, in good condition."

"The ships . . . the ships are probably in disrepair after all this time," said Scorpio.

"The vVos build ships better than that," it said with a dispassionate sort of pride, "but we would of course inspect the vessels to make sure they are up to the voyage."

"Gron, take the ambassador below-ground so that he can look over the ships," said Scorpio.

"I can't believe you're taking that charlatan seriously," Leah said. "To claim that he destroyed an entire world at the snap of a finger—it's ridiculous."

"This is my night sky, not yours," said Scorpio. "I can remember as a fry floating on the waves and looking up at that familiar red disk. It's not there now. But you don't have to take anyone's word for it."

Leah touched the orb at her belt and hesitated as if unsure of whether she really wanted to know. Then she removed the golden sphere and was gone in a bubble of light.

She appeared again so quickly that she occupied the space of her afterimage. For a few seconds Scorpio saw two Leahs, two balls of radiance surrounding her.

The Leah who still stood there when the illusion faded looked sobered. "It's true," she said numbly. "I could only follow the fragments of Hunters' World as they were cast into outer dark. There was wreckage, flames, bodies—"

Scorpio put his arm about her shoulders. "I'm sorry."

"I'm all right," said Leah, attempting to throw off the effects of what she'd seen, "but what are we going to do?"

"That's not really for me to say," said Scorpio. "A decision like this must be made by the Aquay Council, but I'm afraid I will have to report what we've seen tonight. If we Aquay don't send our children, the vVos might destroy our world."

"How can you be sure they'll be satisfied with a thousand of your young?" asked Leah. "What will stop them from sending back more ships . . . and more, and more?"

"Nothing, perhaps," said Scorpio.

"What do you mean, 'perhaps'?" asked Leah. "Do you know something?"

"Only a guess," said Scorpio, "but it's probably a reasonable one. Didn't you say people saw the vVos appear from nowhere, in the middle of a busy street? Think, Leah. Has anyone we know ever done anything similar."

"The vVos must travel by orb," said Leah. "No wonder there was no sign of a ship."

"The Hunters really didn't understand how the orbs worked," said Scorpio, "so they had to have gotten them from someone else."

"This gives us a chance," said Leah. "One orb can track another, so we should be able to follow the ambassador to his planet."

"What we'll find there is anyone's guess," said Scorpio. He was a little surprised and somewhat embarrassed to realize that he was almost relishing the thought of new adventures—after all, there would be no tedious meetings to attend.

Chapter Three

In the Human Compound...

Bone Man crouched behind the cover of a bush with translucent golden leaves and motioned in his economic way for young Chumyip to be silent. A winged creature was dropping out of the sky, the improbable number and flexibility of its wing joints giving it a bizarre shadow against chalky, eroded hills. Its swift descent filled Chumyip with fear. It was much larger than it had first appeared.

At the critical moment, Bone Man unfolded from cover, his lean, dark body uncoiling like a spring. The woomera made a whistling noise as the spear was released.

Chumyip saw that the cast was strong and would have been accurate if the flying creature had not been able to check its descent at the last moment. Its silvery skin-covered wings spread wider, fanning the air as it cut the dive short. Bone Man's spear passed harmlessly below its body. The creature voiced its anger in a screech that made the hair stand up on the back of Chumyip's neck. But, large as it was, the creature did not attack. It rode the air currents, climbing high into the air to escape.

Chumyip watched it on its way, then ran up to where Bone Man stood disgustedly surveying his failure.

"We don't need to hunt anyway," said Chumyip. "There's always food in plenty at the White Grove." He ran to retrieve the spear where it had fallen at the edge of the vast rocky pool. Almost as an afterthought he leaned over, filled a hand with the cool water and brought it to his lips.

When he looked up he saw that Bone Man was watching him in an almost displeased way. "A man always needs to hunt," the old man said stiffly.

Chumyip tried to look properly respectful, but things had gone very strangely on walkabout. He remembered starting out, with the red bulk of Yulara always visible behind them. Bone Man had been expansive, telling tales of the beginning of the world, of the Dreamtime.

A wallaby burst from scrub grass practically at their feet and jumped away in incredible long leaps. Chumyip raised his throwing stick, but Bone Man made a negative sign and said this was a good omen for the walkabout and for Chumyip's coming-of-age.

After a satisfying meal of fat witchetty grubs, they made camp under a boab, but Chumyip did not sleep for a long time. He kept staring up into the stars until a feeling of strangeness stole upon him. He was about to say something to Bone Man when he was blinded by a golden light. Strange, deep voices were trying to speak to him. Since the transformation into manhood was a spiritual as well as a physical journey, Chumyip was not alarmed.

At least not until he awakened the next morning and looked around. "The land is gone!" he shouted, running about in confusion. "Where is the red mountain? Where is Yulara?"

"It's true we may have lost one land," said Bone Man, who seemed to be clinging to mysticism as a kind of defense, "but look, here is another."

This landscape was hardly less bizarre than Chumyip's homeland, but its chalky and crumbling hillsides, stands of golden-leaved shrubs and forests of trees whose boles resembled braided serpents was neither familiar nor comforting. And the air here was chilly, especially since Chumyip wore nothing more than a leather thong. Despite Bone Man's assurances that this must only be a test devised by the gods, Chumyip had a growing horror that they might be walking about indefinitely with no way home.

The clack of Bete Noir's forehoof on stone scattered a half-dozen smaller animals that disappeared into the safety of the underbrush. It also startled one of the monkey men who came suddenly upright, a trickle of water flowing down its chin. Roland le Coeur Hardie saw with a clinical eye that one of those he'd called the monkey men was really a monkey woman a moment before it wheeled and found refuge among the trees.

The creatures puzzled Roland. They had very low foreheads with the hair growing to a sort of topknot. Their mouths looked like the snouts of animals because of the prominent lower jaw, yet there was more than a beast's intelligence in their eyes, and their hands were disconcertingly human. Their scent had driven Noir crazy at first, but he had gotten used to it.

Roland let Noir drink his fill and then put hobbles on the horse's forelegs and set him free to graze. Roland drank and then lay on the grassy bank, his head pillowed in his hands, his sword lying close by. Except for a few puzzles like the monkey men, this place was like the earthly paradise.

An insect buzzed his nose and he slapped at it in annoyance. His mailed gauntlet nearly removed the nose as well. Of course, this place was a little too detailed to be anything other than real.

There had been only the tumult of the battlefield about him when he found himself encircled by a golden light. The shock of it rendered him insensible for a few moments and he awakened here. At first he supposed that he'd been killed in battle and the golden sphere was the Angel of Death coming for him. He was most surprised to see old Noir, his war-horse, encumbered with his full battle gear. He couldn't imagine that horses were admitted into heaven. After a while he was happy about the arrangement, since this seemed a lonely place. After a while he also stopped believing that he had been killed in battle. Obviously he still breathed, ate, slept and thus *lived*.

As he lay there, the scent of unfamiliar flowers sweet in his nostrils, he felt himself drifting off to sleep.

"Sir Knight . . ."

Roland's eyelids felt heavy; he knew he could only be dreaming when he opened his eyes and saw a beautiful dark-haired girl hovering in midair and surrounded by a golden aura. At first he was in confusion, but suddenly he recognized the face. It strongly resembled the painting of the Virgin Mary in the cathedral at Lac du Joie. He was having a vision.

"Our Lady ..." he murmured.

"What are you doing here?" she asked.

"I had hoped you were here to enlighten me."

"This is very strange; I must tell Scorpio," she said.

He saw the film of golden light about her ripple like a candle in a wind and became aware that she was about to disappear.

"Please, Lady. Don't go," he shouted, the sound rousing him from his lethargy. As he sat up and looked around, he saw that the dream vision had dissipated. A new sense of loneliness washed over him. He was sure the vision was caused by his desire for human companionship, but he felt all the more alone now that it was gone.

At first all he could hear was the shuffle of Noir's hoofs on the dry ground, the rhythmic sound of his cropping and chewing of the grass. Suddenly he heard the harsh buzzing as of bees—a whole hive of bees—enormous bees. A shadow crossed him and as he looked up into a smoky-colored twilight sky, he was stunned to see something winged and immense descending.

It was dead black, a clear-cut silhouette as it hovered, suspended on two sets of long transparent wings. The body was sinuous, writhing even as the wings held it aloft, and it had the sinister wedge-shaped head of a serpent, though it was larger than a horse's head.

A flying serpent, Roland thought. Winged lizard.

He heard Noir's full-throated cry of fear.

"A dragon!" he shouted, stumbling to his feet and staggering about the clearing in search of his mount.

The dark lizard descended, anterior wings bringing the tail end to earth a few seconds before the front end. Stumpy legs supported it when it reached the ground, though its sinuous midsection dragged the earth when it walked. Roland had no time to observe more detail. He had found Noir stumbling about in the hobbles. Quickly he removed the hobbles and put the bridle back on. Noir was already in flight as Roland swung to the saddle. All that was necessary was to hang on.

"I have invented a new sin.

"Privacy!

"I, I, I." With each clipped syllable, the hairy long-armed creature danced across the room, speaking its blasphemy into a hand-held recorder.

"The mortals did not wish to keep their bargain, but I overcame them. They made threats, but I only laughed at them. To think they could aspire to kill an immortal such as I

. . . such as the vVos. Imagine them thinking their puny efforts could impede the Great Games!"

Even as the unit played back the tape to listen to its own effusions, it began to feel an overpowering longing. This mission had been a long one and the vVos units were not meant to be away from the cluster that long. The words being played back had a hollow ring; the bravado now seemed only silliness. Impatiently the vVos pulled the tape from the machine, tangling and destroying it.

The unit felt smothered by the heavy body it wore. Abruptly it withdrew its connections and the body dropped to the floor, twitching a little. It lay there as the vVos began to extrude a protective casing and legs. Finally the vVos emerged through an open wound at the back of the creature's neck and hunched there for a half hour more as it unfurled a set of fragile wings and fanned them slowly to allow them to dry.

Just before the vVos was ready to take flight, the sloth-creature began to awaken, moving its arms and legs in a deliberate manner as its rudimentary nervous system regained control of its body. The vVos had found sloths to be perfect hosts. Their well-developed hands were useful in a number of ways. Using sloths, the vVos had created a technological society on Tamir; they had mastered space travel. This had become a necessity in continuing the Games, since most of the indigenous species were now gone.

The brains and nervous systems of sloths operated at such a low level that the arrival and departure of a vVos unit didn't destroy them. Creatures with more developed brains were usually unable to regain control after a possession. Life in the brain and body of a sloth did tend to be somewhat boring, however. Their visual apparatus was limited, as were their emotional capabilities.

Its wings now thoroughly dry, the unit drifted up, leaving the sloth to its own devices, until such time as it needed a host again. The flying unit passed through an open window and rode the blustery wind currents of Tamir, noticing that the world had changed little. It was parklike with its stands of ancient serpent-trees and circular groves of white-trunked boans. Fields of colorful wildflowers tossed in the wind and sent their fragrance upward. The unit did not deviate from its straight-line course to the cluster.

On the wind-blasted hilltop all that showed was a hole amid the rocks where a few winged units hovered, coming and going as they brought water and organic matter to sustain the colony, or, like this unit, returned because there was no other choice.

As the darkness enveloped it, the unit felt the presence of the One. Thought was almost a palpable thing here; it hummed in the shadows like an invisible generator. The pain of separation, of aloneness, began to ebb as it discarded its wings and moved toward the cluster's core.

One by one it cast off its legs and wriggled out of its protective casing. It dragged itself the last few inches to the core, a writhing mass of nerve matter—for lack of a better term, an immense cooperative brain, The One, which existed through time and would not die.

A current of amusement ran through the unit as it remembered its own foolish posturing and declaration of "I, I, I!" What a joke in the face of this completeness. The brief separation no longer mattered as the unit became One. And the whole immense pulsing brain was fixated on one thought: The Games!

Chapter Four

Cradled in the orb-craft, Leah was just as glad she wasn't riding with Scorpio. Orb travel caused them to share thoughts as well, and she wasn't ready to share her failure, even with a friend as close as Scorpio. Orb space offered an opportunity for mental activity. No time passed there and thoughts and memories came instantaneously.

She remembered that she had begun her quest of returning to Earth with high hopes. With so many times and places to choose from, she was sure to find a home.

Leah appeared on a road that was scarcely more than two ruts in a so-far unknown place and time. By the look of the road with forest impinging on it closely, this time was likely to afford lots of serenity, and Leah was ready for that after her travels with Scorpio.

She looked both ways down the road, but nothing was in sight in either direction. Choosing a direction at random, she began to travel down the road. At last it dwindled to what amounted to a cowpath, but she continued to follow the twists and turns until she came at last to a cabin, almost lost amid encroaching foliage. It leaned slightly askew and the logs had weathered to a dull gray. There was a stone coping in front of the house spanned by an iron crosspiece with a handle. Leah went to look over the edge and saw the green gleam of water far below; a scent of moisture drifted upward. Using the rusted handle, she turned until a dented bucket came into view. It brimmed with water. When she drank, she marveled at the coldness and purity.

When she went inside the cabin, sunlight poured in on her through several holes in the roof, but otherwise the structure looked sound. The floor was covered with debris, animal droppings, twigs, broken furniture. Something had nested in the hearth, leaving behind a tangled mass of grass and twigs.

It seems that no one has lived here in a while, thought Leah, so there should be no objection if I move in while I explore this new time.

It took quite a bit of work to make the cabin livable again, but Leah knew all about that. Her life as a physician's daughter in Avignon of 1351 before she met Scorpio had certainly been full of hard work. She was soon settled in, the hearth cleaned and a fire crackling there. Her father had taught her all about plants, medicinal and otherwise, so she had little trouble identifying the edible roots and berries. If there was a settlement nearby, she could add to her larder. But she had been so engrossed in fixing up a home for herself, she had hardly thought of the outside world.

A *home*, she thought, walking about and looking at the cabin. It wasn't a thing of beauty, but she had done what was necessary to make it an adequate shelter. Just the idea of staying in one place for more than a few days thrilled her. *Imagine, no alien enemies chasing me. No orb-jumping out of danger at the last second.*

She was so immersed in her thoughts of stability that she didn't hear the footsteps behind her. When she turned around it was to look into the huge brown eyes of a cow. As a city dweller Leah had had little contact with the beasts, though the farmers did drive cattle about the streets on market day.

Leah wasn't sure at first if she was in any danger, then the beast lowed softly, making her jump back. She turned and ran for the cabin.

When she peered out again, the cow was quietly cropping grass near the well. It didn't seem very dangerous, so she walked near it.

"Oh, you've found Bluebell," said a voice, and a boy about eight climbed the broken fence and ran up to her.

"I didn't exactly find her," said Leah.

"She's been gone all day," said the boy. "We were really worried." The boy bore an expression that was at once childishly sweet and yet solemn, as if with an ancient sadness. He wore ragged garments of brown homespun. It seemed likely to Leah that this might be the only cow the family owned.

"Anyway, she's found." Leah smiled. "Do you want me to help you take her home?"

"No, I can do it." He picked up a branch from the ground and prepared to drive the cow before him. He paused. "I haven't ever seen you here before."

"I haven't been here before," said Leah. "The house was empty, so I moved in."

"You're pretty," said the boy. "I'll tell Mom and Dad that you found our cow." He swatted the cow on the hindquarters and it began to run.

"Wait," said Leah. "What's your name, and is there any settlement near here?"

"I'm Brendan," said the boy. "There's a settlement about two miles over. It's called Salem Village."

Leah watched him go. She wished she had invited him in, shown him what she'd done to the inside of the cabin, offered some fresh berries. She hadn't realized till now, as she remembered his grave, innocent face, how much she needed human companionship. Solitude only went so far. It didn't seem fair to hold in her hands a source of ultimate power, and yet be unable to have the simplest pleasures life afforded—a home, husband, children. She let herself think about Brendan's family. How they might gather happily around the table, sharing their poor fare, yet feeling it was a banquet. It seemed centuries ago that she and her father and Grandmère Zarah had formed a family and shared everything.

She pulled herself up short. It *was* centuries ago and it was in a past she couldn't reclaim, since the orb did not allow travel to times where one might meet oneself.

Leah smiled to herself, thinking that the boy had assumed she had found the cow, when it had only wandered in. *Well, it might make for friendly relations with what must surely be neighbors.*

• • •

A few days later, Leah was glad to see Brendan climbing the fence again. It was a pleasure seeing him play about the yard. He leapt to the top of the well's coping and walked around it, teetering precariously.

"Come down from there," said Leah. "You'll fall." Obediently, he dropped to the ground.

"Do you want some wild strawberries? I picked them fresh," Leah said.

"Sure do," said the boy.

"I'll get some," said Leah, returning to the house.

When she got back, the boy was nowhere in sight. She was angry at first that he had asked her to bring food and then had run away, then she remembered the boy walking along the well's coping.

Grabbing the orb, she activated it and commanded it to take her deep into the well.

Safe inside the bubble, she descended through murky water until she saw the boy's body floating limply. He looked dead. Enclosing him with her in the orb bubble, she brought him to the surface. His lips had turned blue and he wasn't breathing. If she was going to do something, she had to do it quickly. The orb was a healing device, but, as Scorpio had explained, not powerful enough to bring one back from the dead.

When the orb had grown small again, she placed it on the boy's chest where it glowed with a stronger light. A moment later the boy began to cough. She helped him to turn on his side where he coughed out a stream of water.

His flesh was icy to the touch. Leah picked him up and carried him inside. She peeled off his wet clothes and wrapped him in a blanket before the hearth. Soon color began to come back into his face.

"You saved my life," he said as he sipped Leah's herb tea. "I was playing on the edge of the well and then I fell in. I think I drowned. You must have brought me back to life."

"No, I just helped you breathe again," said Leah. "No one can bring someone back to life if they're dead, you know."

"I just felt water pouring in through my mouth and nose, then I didn't know anything," said Brendan. "It felt like dead."

"I'm sure it did," said Leah, "but you just lost consciousness for a while."

She realized that Brendan was looking at her intently. "You're not wet," he said. "How did you save me without getting wet?"

"I did get wet," said Leah. "I just changed my clothes."

"Oh." He looked at her closely again, as if trying to remember what she had been wearing before. She hadn't changed clothes, of course. One didn't get wet when traveling by orb, but Leah began to be a little worried about what Brendan might tell his mother and father about the incident.

In many places she'd been, people were nervous about feats of magic, or feats that seemed to be magic, even if they weren't. So nervous, in fact, that they often killed the ones who did the magic. She hoped she'd convinced Brendan that she hadn't brought him back from the dead. That would certainly qualify as magic in any era. But maybe people here didn't have that problem.

When Brendan was well enough to leave, she worried about what sort of tale he'd bring back home with him. She continued to worry about it for several days, but nothing happened, so her fears were allayed.

One evening she was dozing when she heard the sound of a faint tap at her door. When she opened it, she saw a young woman in clothing even more ragged than Brendan's. She wore her hair bound up in a kerchief. As Leah stood in the open door, the woman looked back over her shoulder in a wide-eyed way that made Leah think of a startled colt.

"What do you want here?" asked Leah.

"My name is Tabitha, servant to the Blaine family. I heard in the village," said the young woman with much stammering, "that you be a witch."

Seeing that Tabitha needed calming, Leah invited her in and began to brew some tea.

"Not everything you hear is true," she said, trying to be cheerful, but secretly afraid. Word was starting to get around.

"They said you found the Palmer's cow, that was lost a whole day, and that you worked some magic to save young Brendan from a fall down a well. I came here to get some help." She looked down as if ashamed, and then continued. "You see, I'm powerful in love with the Blaines' son Timothy, but even though I serve him his meals and clean up after him, he never pays no mind. I guess because I'm just a servant, bound for the next three years because of my father's debts. I figured that if you were knowledgeable about herbs and the like, you could give me something to put into Timothy's food. Something that'd, well"—she smiled selfconsciously and blushed—"make him take notice." She took out something she had tied in the corner of her apron. It was a silver spoon in an ornate pattern. "The Blaines won't miss just one."

"I do have some knowledge of herbs," said Leah, "but my father taught me that aphrodisiacs are sold only to take money from fools. Feelings aren't bought and sold, he would say. If you care about someone, just try to show it. If they care in return, things will work out."

"That sounds wise," said Tabitha. "If you care about someone, just try to show it." She bundled the spoon back into her apron. "I've got to get back."

"I'm sorry I couldn't help you," said Leah as she left.

"Maybe you have," said Tabitha.

Leah had a hard time relaxing in her cabin after this happened because she had an idea that wild stories about her powers were circulating about the village. It wasn't as if she couldn't use the orb to escape, but the point of being here was to establish a home.

About a week later, she saw another woman in a homespun dress and a lace mobcap approaching. The woman detoured around the broken fence instead of climbing it. When she looked into the woman's face, Leah could see a resemblance to Brendan, but the woman was thin and pale, faint traces of a bruise across one cheek.

"I suppose you're Brendan's mother," said Leah, standing on the small porch of the cabin. "Welcome."

The woman stared at the ground for a moment as if too bashful to speak. "I'm Goodwife Palmer, Goodie Palmer," she said at last. "Brendan's mother, as you guessed. I owe you a debt, if what he told us is true."

Leah invited the woman inside. "Brendan has a big imagination," she said when they were cozily installed by the hearth. "What did he tell you?"

"That he fell in the well and died, and that you brought him back to life."

Leah tried to lighten the mood by laughing, insinuating that a boy's tales weren't always true. The woman didn't take the hint. She continued speaking in a serious mood.

"It's all right. I told Brendan he wasn't to tell this to his father, Thomas. I'm married to Goodman Palmer. An upright man." She touched the bruises on her face as if remembering something. "A righteous man. Deacon in the church."

"You shouldn't take the tales of a child so seriously. Brendan exaggerated, that's all. He did fall into the well, but I got him out in time."

"You live alone here," said Goodie Palmer, as if too enmeshed in her own thought processes to hear Leah's explanation.

"Yes, I do," she answered, though she could see no point to the question.

"There used to be a wisewoman, living all alone in a cottage near the village. But she was accused as a witch and hanged in the village square."

"Just because I live alone doesn't mean—" began Leah.

"A woman must be very clever to live without a husband in these times," said Goodie Palmer. "I believe Brendan when he said you found our cow, and that you brought him back to life."

Leah looked alarmed.

"No, don't be afraid," said the woman. "I haven't come here to denounce or accuse you. I've come for your help. Do you see these bruises on my face? There are more that this dress covers." She touched the long sleeve, then the long skirt. "They were given me by Goodman Palmer, Witchfinder

Palmer, as he styles himself. I'm here to buy a poison which I can take to free myself from his cruelty."

Leah was shocked. She had been thinking casually about using the orb to jump out of trouble and feeling sorry for herself because she couldn't stay. This woman wasn't so lucky.

"But what about Brendan?"

"Give me enough for two and he can come with me. If heaven is a better place as we are taught, then all will be well. If not, then we are still better off. I can pay you well. I have kept hidden a bit of money my mother gave me before she died."

Leah talked to Goodie Palmer for a long time, explaining that since she wasn't a witch she couldn't supply any poison. The idea of taking a life made her feel sick, since her father had always taught her to save lives. She also let Goodie talk freely about her life with Thomas Palmer, and to cry openly, and that seemed to release some tension.

"If you don't want to go back, maybe you have some relatives you could go and live with," said Leah.

"No, there's no place else for me," said Goodie Palmer. "I'll have to go back to Thomas. No matter what he's like, it's 'till death us do part.' " She smiled wanly.

Leah felt restless when the woman had left. She supposed she had helped her somewhat, but now it was impossible for her to orb-jump out of the situation without doing something for Brendan and his mother. The problem was she wasn't sure what to do. Inviting them to live here was an attractive idea, but with the tales circulating about her witchcraft powers, they might not be safe here for long.

She took out the orb and looked at it. It was frustrating to be condemned as a witch and not have the powers to go with it. *But I do have powers*, she told herself.

Goodman Thomas Palmer retired that night feeling quite happy with his world. He had denounced that harlot Tabitha for carrying on so publicly with the Blaine boy and then he had chastened his own wife, Constance, and his son. A few blows were unimportant when it came to the safety of their immortal souls. In heaven they would understand that he was the best husband and father possible.

His wife had sobbed silently for some time, but now she was sleeping and all was peaceful. He lay there for a few moments with his eyes closed when he felt a tickling sensation across his forehead. When he opened his eyes, he saw a young woman with long black hair. She was standing over him and tickling his forehead with a long straw.

He lay there paralyzed. The stories about witches said that they came to their victims at night and tormented them, yet most of those who had been victims of witches were hysterical young girls. When they told stories of being pinched and poked in bed, he thought that at least part of it was imagination. Not that there weren't a great many evil women about, but he considered their powers somewhat exaggerated.

He swept the straw aside with one hand and rose from bed as quietly as he could to avoid waking Constance. It would be hard to explain why a deacon of the church was being visited by a witch, especially since he had often said that only the evil drew down the wrath of witches.

"What do you want of me, servant of the devil?" he asked in a hoarse whisper. "My goodness makes me immune to the likes of you!" His face grew red and he looked as if he were about to advance on Leah with violence in mind.

"We'll see," said Leah, waiting until he was close enough to enclose in the orb's aura. They jumped.

The orb bubble hovered over the surface of a live volcano. Leah saw Thomas look down into the bubbling molten rock with his eyes widening. "This is hell," she told him. "If I liked I could drop you down into it to burn for the next thousand years."

Thomas stared into the leaping flames as fumes swept past the bubble's surface. He looked at Leah. All the fight went out of him. "Don't!" he cried. "I will serve you. Yes, I will serve you and your master. I'll do anything you say. From this moment I denounce my church." He danced about inside the orb bubble, as though his feet were already burning, though the orb protected its inhabitants from the fierce heat outside.

"Don't assume things so quickly," said Leah. "There's more." She activated the orb.

The bubble appeared in the vastness of space, an immense backdrop of black scattered with the glowing dust of stars. The view was cold and lonely, but it was also magnificent, as if the whole universe were on display around them. "These are the heavens," said Leah. "You were very quick to wish to serve the devil, remember that, if you wish to cultivate some humility; it's a useful trait."

Thomas looked around at the majesty of the heavens, with no atmosphere to spoil the view. He remembered with chagrin how he had groveled to avoid the heat below. Maybe his own goodness wasn't the powerful talisman he'd always thought it was.

But heaven terrified him even more than hell had, though in a different way. They stood in nothingness, vulnerable and alone. He wished for human contact. Surely this creature with him was other than human, even if she didn't serve the devil as he had thought.

"Please," he said. "Whatever you are, I only want one thing. I want to be home, with my wife and son. I'll serve you, whoever you are."

"You were quick to decide I served the devil," said Leah. "As if the good doesn't also have its messengers. You've heard of guardian angels. Well, I'm one of those. I was sent to earth to guard your wife and your son. So far I have been remiss in my duties, but from now on I'll be watching, *every minute of the day*. I do have the power to take you someplace you won't like and to strand you there forever."

"I believe you; please, take me back." Thomas Palmer began to cry softly.

• • •

Leah stepped from the orb bubble as it landed softly in her own cabin. Goodman Palmer had been overjoyed to see his own home after his travels in heaven and hell, and he appeared to be quite repentant. Still, he might get back to his old tricks eventually. With the orb Leah could be the guardian angel she pretended to be, snapping back into this age whenever it suited her. If Thomas was misbehaving, she could leave him in the Jurassic if she liked.

Her fire had burned to ashes, and she made no move to rekindle it. As much as she had tried to make a home here, she realized it wasn't going to work. The stories told in the village would get wilder and wilder, until people came out to investigate. She couldn't bewitch everyone in the village and she really didn't want to.

She jumped.

In orb space she considered her options, finally deciding to try a more modern age. Maybe ideas of witchcraft would change.

Chapter Five

Leah remembered the commune.

There had been a mound of cushions in the middle of an almost empty room, a splash of sunlight coming through a tall, grimy window. Posters with bright patterns of neon color hung on walls layered in peeling paint. Off in another room someone was playing a repetitive song about a yellow submarine. Leah thought it all rather novel and exciting.

She had arrived in this time ready to scheme and struggle for the basic necessities. That was how it had been in every time period she had visited so far. She had been shocked when a young woman with long, straight blond hair had struck up a conversation and invited Leah to move into the commune. Daffodil, she was called. Daffy for short.

Leah didn't understand the word *commune*, and she was surprised to find that it was an abandoned building. Still, Leah thought, other ages and societies might be richer, but they were not so accessible. She liked the clothes they had given her, a pair of faded bell-bottom jeans and a tie-dyed T-shirt.

"Got a stash?" A cadaverously thin young man with long, greasy brown hair lounged in the doorway. Leah vaguely remembered him being introduced as Slimjim.

Because of the orb's teaching she knew he was referring to pot. The rooms of the old building sometimes reeked with the burning-rope smell.

"Sorry," said Leah, shaking her head.

"Bummer," said Slim and went on his way.

Leah heard excited voices downstairs and made her way down the crumbling staircase. She saw Daffy being supported by several of the commune members. Her skin was pasty white and her long hair was streaked with blood from a crusted wound on her scalp.

"What's the matter?" asked Leah.

"We were at a sit-in," explained the boy supporting Daffy on the right side. "Everything was groovy till the pigs showed up. Then fighting started and some bozo threw a bottle."

Daffy's eyes were glazed over and she made the peace sign with her fingers and waved it drunkenly about. "Bring her up here," said Leah, leading the way up the staircase and kicking cans and other debris out of the way. "Put her down on those cushions and leave her here with me."

"What are you, man, some kind of funky medic?" asked the girl who held Daffy's left arm.

"Sort of. I have a cure I learned from my . . . my grandmother. An old family remedy."

The others left. Daffy lay on the cushions, holding her head and moaning softly. Given her half-conscious condition, she might have a concussion. Hoping that Daffy was far enough gone not to notice the orb, Leah took the glowing sphere from her belt pouch and laid it on the wound in Daffy's scalp. Light pulsed softly, and after a while Daffy stopped moaning. Leah could see that the edges of the cut had drawn closer together. Now all she had to do was to cleanse the wound and everything would be all right.

Because of Daffy's regular breathing, Leah supposed the girl had fallen asleep, but when Leah removed the orb to put it back into the pouch, she saw that Daffy's blue eyes were wide open.

"Oh, wow," she said softly, reaching out for the light as Leah hurriedly shoved the orb into its pouch.

A few days passed, and as Daffy went about her business without mentioning the orb, Leah supposed she had forgotten seeing it, or believed it was only a dream. Leah settled into the life of the commune. Daffy showed her how to panhandle by offering flowers to passersby; Slim was teaching her how to play the guitar.

"Oh, Leah, I'm glad you're here," said Daffy one day as she peered into Leah's room. That wasn't hard to do since few of the rooms had doors. "I've brought someone to see you."

The man Daffy had brought looked out of place and uncomfortable here. He wore a rumpled gray three-piece suit and needed a shave. He thrust a small card into Leah's hand. It said "The National Discoverer."

"The chick tells me you've got some sort of magic," said the reporter.

"Wait a minute," said Leah, taking Daffy aside. "Why did you bring him here?" she asked. "Now everyone will know about the orb."

"So what?" said Daffy. "Nobody believes anything they print in that rag anyway, and besides, he's promised to pay fifty dollars."

Leah supposed she did owe these people something for their hospitality. Grudgingly she took out the orb.

"Yeah, neat trick," said the reporter. "Maybe we can work in an angle about space aliens. My editor is crazy about aliens." He took out a small camera to take some pictures.

Leah felt very vulnerable when Daffy returned a few days later with a stack of newspapers under her arm. Leah was certain that anything appearing in a newspaper was of great importance.

Daffy passed the papers around, handing one to Leah, who saw that she was pictured with a stupid expression on her face as she stared at the orb. The headline read, "Hippies visited by space aliens in UFOs."

Even though Leah was offended by the story the reporter had written, she couldn't help anticipating the arrival of the authorities, coming to investigate the orb. Nothing happened; life went on as usual.

One day Daffy came in again with a flustered, excited look. "Leah, come with me. The greatest thing has happened. We're going to be on a talk show!"

"As in you and me?"

"You, me, and the orb," said Daffy. "Simon Forest reads the tabs to get interesting guests for his show *Simon Says*. I sent him a clipping of your story and we're in."

"Wait a minute. Didn't we watch that show last week? That's the guy who has all the crackpots on so he can make fun of them. He's really nasty."

"Sure, but so what? You know what he pays?"

Leah didn't want to know. Daffy's eyes grew large and unfocused as Leah activated the orb, disappearing in a bubble of light. *Maybe Daffy can go on Simon's show and say she was host to a space alien*, thought Leah disgustedly. *She'd be almost right, at that.*

I guess the only thing worse than being persecuted as a sorcerer is being laughed at for being one, she thought as she jumped to Terrapin.

She could imagine Scorpio's advice—to hide the orb away and never mention it—but what was the point of having such a device if it had to be constantly hidden? At the very least it was there to help her escape a boring and unfruitful age.

It's me, she thought. Someone who has had the ability to move freely from time period to time period isn't going to be happy experiencing time in the usual way.

Her memories were suddenly dispelled as the orb craft materialized. Leah almost panicked as she found herself drifting in space. *The Ambassador has reached his destination,* she thought, *but I must have done something wrong.* As the bubble revolved, she saw a blue and green planet. It might have been Earth except that the configurations of the continents looked so different. *Can that be Tamir?* she wondered. *If it's not, I'm in a lot of trouble.* Hastily, she jumped to the world's surface.

As the orb bubble materialized over an eroded hillside, she was almost relieved to see how alien this place looked. Those trees with trunks like writhing serpents were something that would never appear on Earth, and there were bushes forming a thick-leaved golden canopy beside a rocky pool. Beside the pool stretched a knight, taking his ease. He wore slightly grimy garments and a vest of light mail. His helmet had been cast aside on the grass and a sword lay near his hand. As she stared, he opened his eyes and smiled up at her, though he didn't quite seem to believe what he was seeing.

This is impossible, she thought. I know my mind was wandering in orb space, but the planet I saw wasn't Earth.

When the man spoke, it was in a language close enough to her native tongue that the orb's language teaching was unnecessary. *Why should I have come all this way see someone who might have ridden into Avignon on market day?*

Out of the jumble of her thoughts, Leah remembered that one orb could track another. All she had to do was to get her orb to find Scorpio's.

When Leah ordered the orb to jump, she heard the knight call out to her, and then he was gone, as if he had been only a vision. For a moment, she wondered if she hadn't imagined him there, since she had despaired of ever returning to Earth, but she was too innately practical to doubt herself for long. If she'd seen an armored knight on this alien world, there must be one.

The orb materialized again. While the landscape was similar, it was free of anachronisms, except for Scorpio, who stood looking around in confusion.

"I'm glad you made it," he said by way of greeting. "Did you have a problem?"

"Not really, but I materialized a little too fast. I got a nice view of the planet, though." She was about to tell him about what she'd seen, but it sounded so ridiculous, she decided she'd better wait until she had the proof.

"This isn't what I expected," said Scorpio. "Where are the cities, the technology?"

"Maybe this is a big world," said Leah. "Room for technology and wilderness both. Room for a number of things," she added thoughtfully.

"Maybe so, but we need to find the cities, to see what the vVos society is like." As Scorpio raised his orb, preparing to jump, it began to pulse with prismatic light. Leah saw that her orb was doing the same thing, and before she could stop it, it had fairly leapt out of her hands and was rolling across the ground toward Scorpio.

As he struggled to contain his orb between his hands, the sphere changed shape, literally oozed through his fingers and dropped to the ground. It rolled toward its counterpart.

"Watch out!" Scorpio shouted. "They're going to—" As the orbs came together, there was a burst of light that blinded Leah for a moment. When her vision returned, swimming with golden afterimages, she looked on the ground for the orbs.

"They're gone," said Scorpio. "This happened before. It's their form of mating—or something. When they're brought close enough together, they combine."

"Well, fine, we're stuck here."

"If it happens like last time, the orb will return eventually."

"Let's just hope it happens like last time. I don't like this world *that* much."

"In the meantime, I suppose we're on our own. We need to try and learn something about this world and about the vVos." Scorpio began to walk across a clearing, and Leah followed, but as she approached a line of trees she felt a sudden panic. Her heart began to pound and she was finding it difficult to breathe.

"What's wrong?" asked Scorpio, pausing. "Aren't you coming? You look rather pale."

Leah had backed away a few paces; now she was beginning to feel almost normal again. What had alarmed her? She didn't know.

"I think I'll explore over this way," she said. "We can meet back here in a few hours."

"Well, we could cover more ground that way, if you're sure you're all right."

Leah reassured him and waved him on his way. When he had gone, Leah tried again to pass the line of trees. A surge of fear engulfed her, so strongly that her knees buckled and she fell. Chagrined, she crawled away from the trees. Slowly, her heartbeat and breathing returned to normal. *What's the matter with me?* she asked herself. *First the knight and now this?* She supposed she should have told Scorpio, but he seemed unaffected. He had walked past the trees with no problem. She wasn't sure she could have explained the irrational fears that overwhelmed her when she tried to go in that direction.

Scorpio will be back after a while. I'll try to tell him then, she thought.

Chapter Six

Cnozca rose and walked to the cave's entrance. Darkness hid the land's alien contours, but the patterns of the stars were different. He could hardly bear to look upon them.

In Tenochtitlan each day was carefully charted: seed time and harvest, festivals and days of fasting, seasons of drought and seasons of rain. Everything in his society was carefully ordered so that no god would be left out, none take offense. Now Cnozca was lost in time, each day following the other with no special significance.

Cnozca remembered with regret his handsome clay-brick dwelling, his numerous slaves and his high office as chief priest. He had been anticipating the Festival of Huitzilopochtli, when a captive would be chosen as a sacrifice. The still-beating heart cut from the captive's chest and quivering in Cnozca's hands—was there ever such a feeling of power?

In the days preceding the festival, Cnozca had been permitted to wear the feathered cloak and to carry the ceremonial dagger. He had been wearing them when he had been brought to this place. He still didn't know what offense he had committed to be exiled from his own land, but the punishment was swift and terrible. One moment he had been in Tenochtitlan, looking up at the sacred pyramid where the sacrifice would soon take place, the next he was here. He remembered only a flare of golden light.

It was true he had freedom to move about in this land, but only to a certain extent. When he came to the barrier, he felt the god-touch of fear and could go no farther. It was good to obey the gods, but he had a growing feeling that the gods of this land might not be the gods he knew. It was a feeling that was hard to live with.

He was also being fed, when he could force himself to go to the Circle of White Trees. The hairy god-servants brought food in plenty, though it was nothing like the maize cakes he had enjoyed in his own land. The worst thing about the place was that there were usually others present. Human beings, undeniably, but dressed in outlandish garments and with strange faces. Some had white skins; others were tan or dark brown. Some of the men had large amounts of hair growing on their faces and bodies. Each seemed to be different, and when they tried to communicate, their speech was a meaningless babble. Cnozca was uneasy about these people, not because they were so unlike him but because he suspected that in some way, in committing some crime against whatever gods, he was like them. In the blink of an eye, the status he had worked to achieve over a lifetime had been swept away.

With all these doubts and fears working on him, Cnozca spent most of his time brooding in his cave. On this one particular evening, he backed away from the hateful sight of the stars and returned to the back of the cave, where he built a small fire against the night's chill. He hadn't eaten that day and breathing smoke in the poorly ventilated cave made him feel as if he were floating.

For a moment a shadow blocked the cave's mouth, then a ballooning and insubstantial figure stood over him. The fierce grimacing face, the tall headdress of plumes—

Huitzilopochtli, god of war and the sun. This was a powerful vision; he waited for it to speak.

"You are lost, my son," said the god. "Every day the advancing calendar takes you further from all you have known."

"I have tried to serve you well—I have served all the gods," said Cnozca. "Can't you tell me how I have erred, how I may expiate my offenses?"

"There is one way you might bring your own world close enough to pass through into it again. My festival, the sacrifice—these are things of power. Use this power well, my son."

Cnozca awoke from his trance some hours later with morning's light cold on the stones at the cave entrance. He rose, picking twigs from his hair. The vision was still clear in his mind.

As he looked out of the cave, he saw a rise of land that with a stretch of the imagination one could construe as a pyramid. He still had his feathered cape and obsidian dagger hidden behind some stones at the back of the cave.

All I need now is a captive.

Cnozca set out, feeling more hope than at any time during this ordeal. He heard boisterous singing, though it was in a foreign babble. He stepped behind a screen of brush to see who was approaching.

The crew tramping along the forest trail singing their outlandish song didn't seem likely candidates for Cnozca's needs. There were too many for one thing—eight of them, and all looked to be formidable fighters. Some were armed with immense axes, others with spears, and their faces and bodies bore traces of familiarity with close combat. They had large amounts of facial hair, which Cnozca thought made them look more ferocious, and they wore ragged garments of skin and fur. A few wore helmets of fur and metal with cow horns set to either side.

Cnozca was desperate enough to put up a fight to get his captive, but he was still sane enough to want to stay alive. He let the barbaric-looking men go by and continued his search.

After a while he came upon a small lean-to in the forest. It was camouflaged with branches so he almost overlooked it at first. It had a temporary, yet well-crafted look. A firepit where coals still smoldered suggested that the place was occupied.

Cnozca approached cautiously. No way of knowing what strange being lived here. When he was certain no one was home, he approached more boldly. There was little under the lean-to's roof except two pallets of leaves and dried grasses. On one of the beds lay a strange-looking soft helmet of leather with two round pieces that were obviously used to protect the eyes. Cnozca inspected it and found the craftsmanship amazing.

He found a sack made of some tough material he couldn't place and turned it upside down, spilling out various artifacts. He picked up a square object, like a small box bound in leather. When he opened it, he saw that it was a collection of many square sheets of some light material all fastened together. Some of the sheets had indecipherable markings on them. He turned the object this way and that but couldn't come to any conclusions about it.

He had become so interested in the contents of the lean-to that the first warning of danger he received was an angry shout and the sound of running feet. He looked up to see a figure sprinting toward him. It took a moment for him to realize that it was a woman, since she had short hair and wore close-fitting clothing. She looked tall and strong, but this only pleased Cnozca the more. A fine physical specimen would be more pleasing to the god.

He took a few steps toward her, but she kept coming, still shouting angrily, then she stopped and raised her hand. A tree branch beside his head exploded. Cnozca looked all around, but could find no reason for the explosion. Certainly there was no reason to connect it to the strangely dressed woman who stood some yards away from him. He did notice that she had something in her hand.

With the next loud report, Cnozca was knocked to his knees. When he looked down he saw blood pouring from a wound on his thigh. As he staggered to his feet, he saw that someone else had joined the woman, a man dressed in clothing similar to hers.

He had had enough. He dodged behind the lean-to and began to run, half dragging his wounded leg. There was one more sharp explosion as he zigzagged through the forest, but it never touched him. After a while he allowed himself to stop and listen for sounds of pursuit. There were none.

He was surprised to see that he had gone through all of this with the boxlike artifact still clutched in his hand. He decided it was a magical thing, possibly an amulet of protection.

When he was certain that no one pursued him, he stopped by a stream to wash his thigh wound. He found it wasn't deep; something had only cut shallowly into the surface of the flesh. He still couldn't imagine what sort of weapon had been used.

As Leah walked along she began to feel as if she were being followed. Though she looked behind her several times, she saw no one. Once she thought she heard a soft, chortling laugh, but again when she looked, no one was there. As she negotiated a particularly heavy patch of foliage, she was about to pass under a low-hanging branch when strong hands caught her up under the arms and she felt herself swung off the ground.

She screamed at this sudden attack but seconds later remembered the wrist laser and activated it. Since she was being held, kicking, four feet off the ground, there was no chance of aiming. The beam went arrowing upward and backward. She smelled singed fur and suddenly she was falling. She hit the ground with a thump. Several apelike forms were fleeing through the treetops. She sent a laser bolt after them, but the beam paled and sizzled out. Repeated pressing of the firing stud did no good. The weapon was evidently out of energy and Leah had no idea how it might be recharged.

At least the ape creatures had fled. They might also steer clear of her next time, if their brains were adequate to the task.

She continued walking now with less fear of being harassed from above. Hearing human voices in the distance, she decided to follow the sound. At last she came to a grove of startlingly white trees, even the pennant-shaped leaves snapping in the wind were translucently pale. Though it scarcely seemed as if it could be a natural formation, the trees grew in a perfect circle, looking like the columns of some old temple.

Within the circle Leah saw a fallen tree serving as a long table. Around it were gathered eight barbaric-looking men. Some wore horned helmets and all had bristling beards. They were eating and drinking with gusto as several vVos creatures served as waiters, bringing trays laden with food and drink.

This group wasn't the only one enjoying the vVos's hospitality. Other individuals sat here and there, watching each other suspiciously as they ate.

People, thought Leah. *Earth people. I wasn't dreaming when I saw the knight.* She noted that most of the people were one of a kind: a lean, sunburned man in fringed leather and an odd cap made out of some animal with the tail hanging down in back. A tiny woman with shiny black hair arranged in an ornate style and wearing a shimmering, fluttersleeved garment with a wide sash. Dozens of others, all equally diverse. Many of the men carried weapons, and they looked like they might be fighters. That wasn't the common denominator, however. If there was something all had in common, Leah decided, it appeared to be good health and relative youth. There were no babies or elderly, no one with an obvious sickness. There weren't many folk from Earth's advanced technological ages, she noticed. Perhaps their pampered lives left them less robust. She remembered the vVos ambassador's demands of the Aquay: one thousand swimmers in the best physical condition. With this demand, the Aquay had assumed the vVos were planning to eat their young.

Leah watched the vVos passing out food, and wondered if these people were only being fattened, like cattle for the slaughter. The thought sickened her. When a vVos approached her with his tray, she saw that the bowls on it contained a white, cereal-like stuff. The drinking vessels held a golden liquid.

With the thoughts she'd been having, she drew back and made a gesture for the creature to go away.

"Very well. Food and drink will be here when you want it," it said in that nasty, glutinous voice. "No doubt you will be hungry soon."

Leah stared as it shambled away, surprised that it had spoken to her in the language of the Aquay. Considering that the vVos had orbs, it wasn't so surprising that their ambassadors and other high-ranking individuals would be fluent in many languages. She did find it strange that even the servants shared this trait.

None of the Earth people appeared to be able to communicate with each other except those who had, for some reason, been brought in groups.

The puzzle was too much for Leah. It was all too bizarre. The vVos certainly did not intend to banquet on these people—a great deal of trouble had evidently been taken to bring them here from all ages of Earth's past. If it were only a matter of meat, it could have been arranged much more easily.

Though many of the people looked barbaric, behavior was surprisingly good in the grove. Leah understood why when a man with a long, drooping mustache and ornate, lacquered armor began to leap about, brandishing a sword and shouting. The object of his anger, a man in fringed leather, laconically drew a long-bladed knife.

Two of the vVos creatures hurried up, each carrying something in its hand that was too small for Leah to identify. She saw the angry combatants give way before the vVos. One fell to the ground; the other began to run. She couldn't be sure, but she thought the men might be reacting to the same kind of irrational fear that had blocked her from leaving before.

Once the disturbance had been quelled, eating and drinking began anew. It was as though nothing had happened.

Feeling that there were still mysteries here that she hadn't solved, Leah decided to move on. She squinted at the sun and realized she should retrace her path to rejoin Scorpio. Maybe he had found something to help solve the riddle of this place.

Returning to the spot where she had left him, she waited for a long time, but Scorpio didn't arrive. Since she couldn't pass the boundary marked by the trees, she couldn't very well go looking for him. At least she now knew a device of some sort caused the fear, but knowing that wouldn't stop the effects.

Night began to fall. It was growing chilly, so Leah decided to seek shelter. She hoped Scorpio might return in the morning. She walked along, following a stream. At least wherever she decided to stay, she would have drinking water. The stream ended in a sinkhole, a patch of stinking, bubbling mud.

She noticed a rocky overhang on the hillside above and thought it would make good shelter. Laboriously, she climbed up to it and crept inside out of the cool wind.

It was dark, so she felt her way to the back of the overhang, crawling on hands and knees because the rocky ceiling was so low. Suddenly she felt warm flesh beneath her hands and someone let out a shriek.

Chapter Seven

Hatshepsut fidgeted as her handmaidens helped her put on her finest dress of gauzy pleated linen with its matching golden collar and anklets. It was a fine day outside and usually she could find a time to slip away from court affairs to wander along the Nile, sometimes even to spear some fish. But the court had been in a buzz since the death of the boy-king Amenhotep. Plans were being made for an immense funeral.

Although Hatshepsut and Amenhotep were cousins, she didn't know him well. Occasionally she had gone out with him on the royal barge, always with a large group of relatives. She remembered one particular time when she had been sitting beside him as he sat on a gold-encrusted chair, slaves shading him with giant fans or deftly waving the insects away from his royal presence.

• • •

He looked foolish, she thought, surrounded by all this pomp, a crown perched on his small head. "Cousin Hatshepsut," he said, "look over there." When she looked there was the familiar shape of a pyramid at some distance on the horizon. This one was as yet incomplete. Workers toiled away, looking at this distance like ants from a broken anthill.

"That is my tomb," said Amenhotep. "It will be the largest in this region."

Hatshepsut felt a thrill of fear to hear him talk about his tomb in such a matter-of-fact way. Of course, she had been taught that if all were done correctly in the funeral rites, the dead went to another place beyond the Western Sea, where the sun, the boat-of-thousands-of-years, sank every evening after its travels across the heavens.

She supposed an afterlife must be comforting to someone old, but she preferred the warmth of the sun on her back and the caress of the water on her bare legs as she waded into the tepid river among the reeds. She always watched carefully for crocodiles, but they were usually sated from the abundant fish.

Life interested her, not death, so she wasn't sure what to say when Amenhotep so proudly showed her his future resting place.

"Do you like it?" he asked.

And since he was the king, she replied, "It's more beautiful than all the others. It must be comforting to know you will have such a fine resting place."

"You will also have a fine resting place, Hatshepsut," Amenhotep said, as though he wished to please her.

"Yes, my family is wealthy and our tombs will be fine as well, but of course they can't compete with a royal pyramid." She felt a sense of unreality, talking of subjects she had no interest in. But since she had been raised at court, she could often hold forth at length on any number of ridiculous topics. A spear in her hand and a darting fish in her sights, that was more like it. If she had been of greater rank, she wouldn't have been allowed such freedoms, but her mother dead, her father much occupied at court, she found it easy to elude her keepers. As she grew older, she also grew more clever.

"Have you heard any rumors as to what my father wishes to speak to me about?" asked Hatshepsut.

"We are slaves, Highness, and hear nothing of importance," said Quenna.

"I've heard you chattering when you think I can't overhear," said Hatshepsut. "Nothing in the court is safe from a slave's ears."

"A slave's ears or tongue isn't safe when it comes to royal secrets," joked Quenna.

Convinced she wasn't going to learn anything that way, Hatshepsut sat impatiently until the grooming was finished.

When she was ready, she was conducted to her father's private chambers, accompanied by her handmaidens and several men she recognized as hangers-on at court used as go-betweens by her father. Something of importance was about to happen, but she didn't know whether to be happy about it or not.

Khafre, her father, was pretty much a stranger. She would see him on court occasions. He would admire her and say how well she was growing, then forget her until the next time. She was used to it by now, so it caused her little grief. Having no one to supervise her except handmaidens and slaves, she was more free to go her own way.

Today Khafre was sitting in a chair with silver lion heads at the end of each arm and feet like lion's paws. No one sat on chairs except royalty or near royalty.

He was a handsome man except for his dark eyes that were close-set and a little too intense. Hatshepsut had discovered long ago that Khafre was incapable of an expression of true warmth. What he had was a sort of ingratiating mask. He had the mask on now as she entered.

"My daughter, how well you've grown," he said predictably.

She bowed her head in subservience as she knew a good daughter should. Instead of asking why he'd sent for her, she stayed silent, though she was bursting to find out. These were the sort of manners expected of an obedient daughter.

"I have something of great importance to say to you," he said. "It involves a secret we must keep and a great honor that is to be bestowed upon you. You know that Amenhotep, our pharaoh, is dead of a sudden fever. It is a great pity. I believe you knew him, a fine boy."

Hatshepsut wished he'd get to the point. It was so difficult listening to him mouth platitudes. Maybe others in the court would think they were true, but she didn't.

"I knew him a little," said Hatshepsut. "He was my cousin and I sometimes accompanied his entourage on state occasions. He seemed very . . . nice," she said, thinking a bit of praise for the dead not out of place.

"Amenhotep's death was sudden, and his family would not have him go alone into the grave; they don't feel it is fitting for a great pharaoh. So his family and I will announce that long ago you and the Pharaoh were secretly betrothed. The funeral service and the marriage will coincide. You will be Queen of Egypt."

Hatshepsut was at first confused by her father's labyrinthine plans. Being Queen of Egypt might seem like a great honor and she was momentarily flattered. But when she considered the rest, she could no longer remain silent. "If the marriage and burial are held simultaneously, that means I'll be dead."

"It is a great honor," said Khafre. "Your name enshrined throughout history. A fine house for the afterlife, with all the treasures Amenhotep has amassed. You do believe that life continues beyond death, do you not?"

"Of course I believe it," said Hatshepsut. She didn't add that the afterlife was something she had intended to experience much later in this life.

"Then all is well," said Khafre. "We will prepare for the ceremonies at once."

He looked away, thus dismissing her from his presence.

Hatshepsut was numb as she walked from her father's chambers. She cursed at a handmaiden who tried to straighten a fold in her dress. *I have to get away*, she thought. *I can't think in this confining place.*

A few hours later she walked along the Nile with her small fishing spear over her shoulder. She had not changed from the delicate gauzy dress, but in her frame of mind she didn't even think about it getting soiled and ruined. *The old schemer is going to have me killed*, she thought, *to advance himself*. She guessed that her betrothal to Amenhotep meant a nice sinecure for her father in the royal court. She was sure he wouldn't have bothered, otherwise.

If my father's men come for me, I'll give them this—and that! she thought, jabbing the fishing spear about fiercely.

The river was particularly beautiful today. Golden reeds arched over blue water and farther offshore she could see hippopotami lazing along, submerging and coming to the surface with satisfied grunting noises. *Mother Nile*, Hatshepsut thought. *How can I give you up to go sleep under stones? If I continue to walk along your length for miles, I could live off the fishes I speared. Sleep farther up the bank under logs or in caves. Make my own way in the world.*

Even as she created this daydream, she saw how foolish it was. She had never raised a hand to prepare food or even to dress herself. She'd certainly die in the wilderness. After her walk it was inevitable that she would return to her quarters and await word about the impending wedding and funeral.

As she lingered on the bank, she thought the sun came from behind a cloud because gold spangled her eyes. When she recovered, she felt that she was flying. *Ra has taken me for his bride*, she thought. *I am riding the boat-of-thousands-of-years high above the earth*.

Overcome by this new development and all that had gone before, Hatshepsut fainted.

When she awoke she was lying beside a stream. For a moment she thought that the Nile had shrunk to this small rivulet, then upon studying the landscape saw no reeds, no hippos, not even any crocodiles. She would have been ecstatic to see a crocodile at that moment. By some act of a god, she had been transported to this strange land. She remembered that she had been wishing to run off to be by herself and make her own way. *It was not a good idea to make wishes where a god might overhear*, she thought.

Chapter Eight

In the darkness of the cave, Leah felt someone grappling with her. Her first impression was that she had startled someone human, but a moment later she wasn't so sure when she felt sharp teeth clamped to her forearm.

Leah yelled in pain and pummeled her enemy, but it seemed the jaw-grip couldn't be broken. Half crazed with pain, Leah rolled over and over, carrying her antagonist with her. The grip was broken as they both began to roll down the slope. Leah felt certain she'd be injured when they reached the bottom.

Her fall was abruptly broken by something as soft and yielding as a bed. The sulfurous stink told her she had fallen into the mud of the sinkhole.

As she sat up moonlight showed Leah her opponent. It was a girl who looked a little younger than herself. The girl was slightly smaller, but her body was wiry and muscular. She had almond-shaped eyes and light brown skin and wore a pleated dress of some thin material. Now the garment was blotched by mud.

The girl looked down at herself and then at Leah and said something that Leah didn't understand. By the tone, it wasn't a compliment.

"How was I to know you were there?" asked Leah, releasing anger in words, even though she knew they wouldn't be understood. "You scared me, too, and why did you bite me? I'll probably be poisoned, you . . . serpent!" She displayed the bleeding wound.

The girl spat out a few more words that sounded like curses. When Leah didn't react, she picked up a handful of mud and threw it straight into Leah's face.

Leah wasn't slow to respond, grabbing a double handful of mud and delivering it square in the front of the girl's once-immaculate dress. Mud flew thick and fast for a few minutes, but after a while, they both stood back, panting and looking at the mess the other had become.

Leah wasn't sure who started laughing first, but it was contagious. Both laughed until their sides hurt at the spectacle of the other and the absurdity of the situation. Obviously, there could be little communication except for the shared laughter. With many miscues, they managed to exchange names. Leah discovered that the girl's name was Hatshepsut. After a while, they helped each other out of the sinkhole. Leah pointed downstream and made washing motions.

When each had bathed and was clean again, they climbed the hill exhaustedly and shared the shelter of the overhang for the rest of the night.

When Leah awoke, Hatshepsut was still sleeping peacefully, so she decided to go back to the stream for a drink of water. She returned just in time to see a crouching silhouette slip in under the overhang. There was little about to serve as a weapon, but she picked up a sharp-edged rock and approached cautiously.

When she heard a scream and sounds of a struggle, she abandoned caution and began to run. As she reached the overhang, the intruder was just coming out, dragging

Hatshepsut with him. In the excitement of the moment, Leah could tell little about him except that he was bronzed-skinned and had an odd profile with receding forehead, large nose and foreshortened chin. He wore a headband about his straight dark hair and a short, skirt-like garment.

Hatshepsut had her hands bound behind her, and didn't seem to be even attempting to struggle.

Leah leapt forward. The intruder was much larger than she was, so she didn't want to give him a warning, but unfortunately stones rattled beneath her feet. He whirled about, just in time to dodge the blow she had aimed at him. He dropped his captive and grabbed Leah's arms. He heaved.

A moment later Leah was hurtling down the hillside, this time on the opposite side, so that she landed on hard ground rather than in soft mud. She lost consciousness briefly, then sat up, rubbing a bump on her forehead. When she had determined that there was no greater damage, she remembered Hatshepsut and struggled to her feet.

When she had reached the hilltop again, she looked out across the landscape and saw two figures, one dragging the other along. She looked about for her edged stone, and then decided that the intruder was more than a match for her. If she was going to do anything, she had to have help. The White Grove wasn't that far away and she could be pretty sure to find someone there, since they would be hungry after the night's fast. The only thing she couldn't be sure about was if she could make someone understand her problem. Still, it seemed the only thing to do. She turned in that direction and began to run.

When she arrived at the circle of white trees, she saw that she had been right. Several people lounged about and the vVos continued their feeding chores. Leah scanned the possibilities: a woman with jet-black skin wearing a scrap of cloth about her middle and carrying a long spear, two men in long-tailed red coats with a multitude of brass buttons. The main problem would be communication. After her time travels in the orb, she did have a fund of several languages that had not left her, but she couldn't be sure who spoke what language. As she looked farther, she saw a horse grazing among the trees and at only a little distance the knight.

As Leah hurried up to him, he looked first surprised and then his expression changed. Leah couldn't be sure, but he looked almost worshipful as he made a low bow to her. "Lady, I didn't expect to see you here, like this."

Leah wanted to ask him what he meant by "like this," but there really wasn't time. "I need your help," she said. "A companion of mine was carried off by a strange-looking man. I tried to help her, but I wasn't strong enough to overcome him. He threw me down the hill." She supposed her torn clothing and scraped skin was obvious testimony to this, though she hadn't really thought of her appearance.

"Blasphemy!" said the knight, "though it's hard to think of Our Lady taking part in vile combat."

"I think we still may be able to save her, but we have to hurry," said Leah.

"Roland le Coeur Hardie at your service," said the knight hastily, looking around for the horse. He located it and ran over to mount.

"I will ride behind you," said Leah, "and show you where they were headed."

The knight looked puzzled, yet put down his hand to pull her up behind him, and they set out.

"Can't you ride faster," she yelled over his shoulder as the horse trotted from the grove.

"I fear for your safety," said Roland.

"I'm able to hold on," said Leah, grasping him firmly about the ribs. His indrawn breath told her that he was shocked or unsettled by her action, but this wasn't the time for dainty sensibilities. "Go, go!" she urged.

Roland spurred the horse and it settled into a lope, covering the ground quickly. Leah directed Roland to the place she had last seen Hatshepsut and her kidnapper.

"There they are!"

Leah could make out two figures just reaching the top of a barren hill. Roland urged Noir forward. Leah breathed more deeply; Hatshepsut was still alive. She hadn't been sure what she would find.

Cnozca was happy as he urged his captive up the hill. She had been hard to handle at first, but exhaustion had taken the fight out of her. He wondered if he should have also taken the second woman captive, in case there was something wrong with this sacrifice. He had been so intent on his plans, he had just cast her aside. Still, this captive looked quite acceptable, and he might even have killed the other when he threw her into the rocks. He hadn't bothered to see.

He reached the top and looked around. An irregular but flat-topped large stone he had noticed was perfect as an altar. He had prepared things earlier by hiding the feather cloak and the sacrificial knife in a hollow beside the rock. He lifted the captive and lay her across the stone. She was asking him something, but he didn't know what. It didn't matter; soon she would be with the gods, and hopefully, he would be back with his people. He stooped to put on the cloak and to retrieve the knife.

The girl started to scream when she saw him approaching, knife in hand, but since she was bound, she could not escape. He raised both hands and began with a short prayer to Huitzilopochtli. Nothing could be left out; everything must be perfect.

Cnozca heard a sound as he tore the captive's dress down the front. Pounding, rhythmical, the sound wasn't one he could place. It nagged at him as he tried to maintain his concentration. There was little left of the ceremony except to cut into the chest and extract the beating heart.

The sound came nearer, and Cnozca couldn't resist looking over his shoulder to see what it was. A tall beast, the like of which he had never seen, threeheaded, eight-limbed, came hurtling toward him. He made a feeble effort to defend himself with the sacrificial knife as the behemoth drew nearer, but its weight bore him down and one of its huge, hoofed feet hit the dirt inches from his head. As it passed over him, he leapt to his feet and began to run.

Leah watched the madman run headlong down the hillside, not bothering to detour around thorny bushes or piles of rock. Feathers torn from his cape fluttered in the air behind him.

"Shall we give chase, Lady?" asked Roland, reining back the eager horse.

"No, I guess not," said Leah. "It doesn't look like he'll be back. I want to see if Hatshepsut is all right."

Hatshepsut had struggled off the stone and was still fighting to free her hands when Leah reached her. Her dress was torn and she was sobbing, but she didn't appear harmed otherwise.

Leah worked at the knots until they came loose. She still couldn't understand what Hatshepsut was saying, but at the moment it seemed enough to tie together the front of her torn dress and comfort her until her crying stopped. She still had no idea why the man had attacked them, unless he really was a madman. If the Earth folk were here long enough, they would eventually learn each other's languages or a common way to communicate, but until that time there were bound to be clashes of cultures. Leah wished for the orb, but it would return to Scorpio in its own time, or not. She couldn't count on that; she had to find a way for herself and her friends to survive here on her own.

"She seems to be unharmed," said Roland.

"We were lucky to have come in time," said Leah, helping Hatshepsut to her feet.

"I would have expected no less since You took an interest in her rescue, Lady. Is she a good friend of yours?"

"I just met her," said Leah, "and we don't even speak each other's language, but yes, I think after all this we're friends."

"Your charity is well known in the world of men," said Roland. "I apologize if I acted strangely before. It's just that I didn't expect to see You as You are. Er, looking like a real person, I mean."

Leah looked at him, puzzled. Then she remembered that the first time he had seen her was in the orb bubble, when he had stared at her, entranced. No wonder he might have considered her a dream or vision. That explained his confusion when he saw her in the White Grove, bloody and disheveled, with no orb to give luster to her appearance.

"I'm quite real," said Leah with a smile, "as you can see. And very grateful to you."

"Maybe we should take your friend back to the grove," Roland suggested. "She can get something to eat, and no one will bother her there."

"That's a good idea. I noticed that the vVos enforced the peace there, if nowhere else."

"When there's time, you must tell me about this place," said Roland. He laughed softly. "When I first came here, I thought I had been killed in battle, and that this was heaven. Still, with You here, perhaps it *is* heaven."

Leah smiled. It was a nice compliment, but he seemed quite intense when he said it, as if it somehow meant more than just an expression of courtly love. Leah had to admit she was beginning to find him attractive, though this was probably not the right time or place.

They boosted Hatshepsut to the horse's back. Roland offered his hand to help Leah mount also, but she declined. "We can't all ride," said Leah.

As they started out, Roland stumbled over something lying by the flat stone. "What's this?" He bent to retrieve the object. It turned out to be a small leather-bound book. He opened it clumsily with gauntleted hands.

"Be careful, you'll tear it," said Leah, taking it from him. She opened the pages more carefully and saw that there was handwriting inside. She closed it quickly. "The madman must have dropped it. We'll take it with us and maybe it'll give us a clue to his behavior."

Chapter Nine

When they returned to the grove, few humans remained there. As Leah sat at the long log table with Hatshepsut, she remembered her own hunger. A vVos appeared, setting a tray of food before them. It was the same dish they had served before and tasted as bland as it looked. Still, the vVos had been right. Eventually, everyone became hungry. She began to eat almost eagerly. When she looked up, she found Roland staring at her in surprise.

"You look shocked. Are my table manners so bad?"

"Your manners are, of course, exquisite, Lady. I just didn't expect—"

She remembered he still considered her some sort of unworldly vision, so no wonder he was surprised to see her stuffing her face like anyone else. Eventually he'd figure it out, she supposed, and these awkward moments wouldn't occur.

When she had finished eating, and Hatshepsut seemed much more composed, Leah asked Roland to accompany her a little farther from the grove, so she could have quiet to study the book they had found. He led her to a spot behind a screen of foliage, where the sunlight came through in shifting patterns. There they settled themselves against a grassy bank, and Leah opened the book.

"Log: Around the World Flight, 1937" was written across the top of the first page. Leah was surprised to find it was written in American English. Her last trip to Earth had taught her this language, but this was written with much jargon and many technical words. The problem with the orb's teaching was that it provided all the words without the corresponding experiences to go with them, so she sometimes knew words that meant nothing at all. That was the case here. Unable to figure out much, she leafed through the book. Everything in the first part was written in tight little letters, but on the last pages, the words were sprawled across the page, as if written hastily. It also became more understandable.

This book can no longer serve as a log of our flight, but I will continue it as a journal of our experiences, which are somehow beyond the ordinary. If worse comes to worst and we do not return, perhaps someday this book will be found.

We took off July 1 from New Guinea on our way to Howland Island, but somehow we got off course and lost radio contact. When the golden lights appeared, I asked Fred if he had ever seen a similar phenomenon on a flight, but he was as puzzled as I. Then the light enveloped us, and strangely, we were floating outside the plane, near the starboard engine. We were buoyed up by the light, and there was a figure beside us, something not exactly human with long arms and a small head. The Lockheed began to wobble and lose altitude. Finally it nose-dived toward the ocean. Shock must have made me black out, because the next thing I remember is awakening to find myself lying under a tree.

I told Fred that things didn't look right here, but he said that we must have crash-landed on an uncharted island and wandered away from the plane. Delirium was the cause of our odd memories. He suggested we search the island for wreckage after we've rested and built a temporary camp.

We will survive because we've found water, and I have my revolver to bring down small game. I hope Fred is right, but those old tales pilots used to tell about flying saucers keep coming back to me. I used to think of them as jokes, to fool the newcomers, but now I begin to wonder . . .

That was how the last entry ended.

"Is it of great moment, as you thought?" asked Roland.

Leah looked up. She had been so engrossed in the experience of the aviator, she had almost forgotten the knight. He had evidently been watching her with worshipful eyes all the time. She smiled at him, which seemed to somehow disconcert him, though at his age he couldn't be such an innocent as that.

"I don't think it has anything to do with the madman who attacked us. It must have been dropped there by someone else. I'll keep it in case we run into its owner."

"Very well, Lady," he said.

"This spot you found is very pleasant," she said. "Secluded." She moved a little closer to Roland and lay her hand near his, so that he might more easily reach out for it.

He cleared his throat noisily and tried to ignore her gesture. In her life in the fourteenth century, Leah would scarcely have dared be so bold, but travel through time had showed her that what was proper varied age to age. She took Roland's hand in hers and looked up at him in a way that the callowest youth could not mistake. Their eyes met, but Roland turned away first. "Lady, please. This is impossible. I'm completely unworthy."

"Unworthy of me, just because you first saw me in what you considered a vision?"

"Yes, because I saw You in your heavenly splendor. Because You are the Virgin."

Leah now drew back. "That is not a thing to speculate about openly, Sirrah."

"I didn't say 'a' virgin," said Roland. "I said 'The.' "

It took Leah a few seconds to sort out what he was saying. When she did, she began to laugh.

"What amuses you?" asked Roland.

"Only that you've made a terrible mistake. I'm not who you think I am. I'm not the Virgin Mary."

"You're not?" Roland seemed immensely relieved. "But you so strongly resemble the painting in the cathedral, and there was the golden halo. I thought—"

"Any resemblance to a painting is an accident," said Leah. "And the golden light can be explained, though I think I'll save that for another day."

"You're not," Roland said, now reciprocating her advances and going them one better by taking her into his arms. "Of course you aren't. What a great fool I was! But this place is so strange. A man might come to believe anything here."

They hugged happily for some moments, then Roland said, "We must exchange tokens as an expression of our feelings." He reached under his shirt and drew out a silver pendant on a golden chain.

"The medal of Saint Christopher, patron of travelers. May it protect you in your travels." He put it gently about Leah's neck. "Now you must pledge to me."

Leah looked down at herself. She wore no jewelry and carried no amulets. She saw that the laser weapon was still clamped to her wrist like a shiny, black bracelet. It was useless for its original purpose, since the power had failed, but would make a reasonably good token. She released the catch and took it off her arm. It fit Roland's wrist as well as hers, so cunning was the Hunters' craftsmanship.

"That looks strange," said Roland. "What is it?"

"This is a powerful love charm," she said. "Whenever you touch this button our love is reaffirmed and made new."

They lingered in their hideaway for a bit longer, talking pleasantly, making vague plans for the future. "Do you know another reason I thought it was so funny you confused me with the Virgin," said Leah. "She and I are of the same religion. We're both Jews."

Roland's expression went, all in a moment, from warm friendliness to utter cold. "I am a Christian knight," he said. "Jews are Christ killers, a hated people!" He stood, pushing away from her, then turned his back on her.

Leah was surprised at his reaction, yet down deep she had not forgotten the feelings of medieval folk toward the Jews. Roland may have been torn from his own land, but he had brought his belief system with him. Leah remembered that when she had first been carried away by the orb, she determined that she would keep her own identity and beliefs as she moved from era to era. Bouncing around in time had given her a new appreciation for compromise, but Roland wasn't ready to amend his beliefs yet.

Leah got to her feet and stumbled away, as tears blinded her. She should have asked for help from anyone other than Roland. Her own time was not ready for her and she had rejected it in turn. *So why do I flee to the first representative of the fourteenth century I see?*

Scorpio was right when he had told her that time travelers only hurt themselves when they reached out for comfort from the time-bound. When Scorpio had told her that, his face had held a deep sadness, as if he knew this from experience.

When she had finally gained more control of her emotions, Leah took hold of the chain about her neck and broke it, letting the medallion drop into the dirt as she walked on. She had to become more practical. What she had told Roland was nothing more than romantic twaddle. The bracelet would hardly affirm anything, even if he did press the firing stud as she directed. He would most likely cast aside the token anyway, as she had discarded his gift.

I'm not here to indulge myself in romantic dreams, she told herself. *Scorpio and I have our mission to find out why the vVos are collecting sentient life-forms.* She continued to walk more purposefully than before, but something had gone out of the day. Tamir's sun was high and cold, more alien than before.

When Scorpio left Leah, he walked toward a dark outline on the horizon that he supposed was a mountain chain. Distances were deceptive and he wasn't sure he could reach them in the few hours he had before he was supposed to meet Leah again, but he might reach the foothills. The higher ground might help him locate signs of the civilization he knew had to be here. Tamir might look like a wilderness, but the vVos had not developed orbs, spaceships and planet-buster bombs under a tree.

He trudged along steadily until the ground began to be broken with black outcroppings of rock and the hills became steeper and more jagged. He studied the torturous trail ahead and wondered if it was as dangerous as it looked from here. There should just be time to reach the nearest summit for a better look at the surrounding countryside before he had to turn back again.

Leah's decision to go off on her own nagged at him. He had accepted it readily enough because after their travels together he was confident she could take care of herself, even on an alien world. It was also next to impossible to change her mind once it had been made up. Still, she had looked strange—pale and frightened. It was almost as if she feared to follow him. Since that made no sense, he tried to put it from his mind, but he found himself worrying about her anyway.

He had climbed almost halfway up, the sun hot on his shoulders, when he saw something sitting on a narrow ledge. It was an ellipse with a purple-blotched, leathery shell ... an egg of some kind? What parent could think so little of its young to abandon an egg here this way? As he watched, it began to roll about. Something was about to hatch from it, but Scorpio saw that the young one was very likely to roll off the edge in its struggles, ending its life before it had a chance to be born.

As the egg teetered on the edge, Scorpio ran the last few yards and caught the egg, just as it was about to go over. He cradled it and watched as a section of shell was pushed out. A skinny black foreleg emerged and waved about. Whatever it was, it wasn't going to be a beauty.

Scorpio was about to put the egg back on the ledge, but he hesitated, curious as to what sort of thing was emerging. A blunt black head was now poking from the shell. Scorpio would have noticed the thunderous flapping noise much sooner if his attention hadn't been on the hatchling, but now he heard it and looked up. A huge shadow was descending on him. It was an incredible creature, a sinuous black lizard held aloft on two pairs of transparent wings. Obviously, what Scorpio held was its young, and the egg had not been abandoned at all. In fact, the mother had stayed around to protect her hatching egg.

Scorpio backed up slowly and, with great care, placed the egg at the back of the ledge. Perhaps the thing was intelligent and would know by Scorpio's movements that he meant the young one no harm.

The lizard just hovered there, creating a wind with its wings. Feeling he had a chance to escape, Scorpio began to descend the trail. Before he'd taken ten paces, the lizard swooped on him, almost knocking him off the narrow rocky hill. He broke a branch from a thorny bush and used it as a weapon to keep the lizard at bay as he tried to make his way to safety.

For a while it worked, the lizard staying at a distance as he descended, but when he had to negotiate a sharp turn, he slipped and had to reach for handholds. The branch dropped from his hands.

Seeing an opening, the lizard darted in and grasped Scorpio in its talons. He felt the sharp claws penetrate his skin and then he was being lifted.

The ground gave way with dizzying speed, and Scorpio wondered what destination the lizard might have in mind. A minute later he screamed as he felt the talons release their hold. The ground was his only destination and from this high up, he wasn't likely to survive the landing.

The first few yards of his fall were almost exhilarating as he plummeted, then he went end over end and the ground sped toward him like a juggernaut.

Chapter Ten

He had closed his eyes, but now he felt a tremendous jerk as if he had been stopped in midair. When he opened his eyes, he saw that was exactly what had happened. Another flying creature had caught him with almost handlike appendages, and now it was attempting to swoop upward with the added burden of his weight. He almost couldn't follow the movement of long, strangely jointed wings covered with white skin. This close, he could see that the white wings and long-furred body were marked in white-on-white patterns, stripes and whorls and blotches.

With an effort, the flyer was moving steadily upward with Scorpio dangling beneath. Scorpio was glad to be saved, but couldn't be sure that this wasn't some sort of game between two species of flyers. Catching the victim at the last minute might be their idea of sport, and perhaps he was only being carried higher to be dropped again.

His mind was put at rest when the flyer veered high over the mountains and descended toward an intricate construction fastened between two cliffs of black rock. From above it resembled a spider's web; it had the same gauzy symmetry, but when they got closer he saw that the struts were of braided cord and looked very solid. The center was woven into a sort of pouch, and it was in here that Scorpio was deposited. The flyer swooped away.

The pouch was like a tiny, swinging room, not uncomfortable since the bottom was lined with soft down, probably plucked from the flyer's body. When he climbed up to the opening and thrust out his head, the sight of the open canyon below made him dizzy. A river was a bright thread moving through dark foliage. The cords of the flyer's web radiated away in all directions, and it might be possible to climb out on one and follow it to the cliff's edge where the strands were connected.

Scorpio grasped one of the cords and began to pull himself out of the nest, but a gust of wind set the whole thing swinging, and he had to retreat. He would just have to wait and see what the flyer had in mind for him.

Cnozca brooded in his cave, nursing his wounds. It had not been as easy to obtain a captive in this land as he had thought it would be. Still, there were lots of people about, and it was only a matter of time until he got his hands on the right one.

As he sat there contemplating his chances of returning to his own land, a winged creature flitted in through the cave's mouth. Downy and gray, its wingtips edged with azure. It wasn't as bright colored as some of the other insects on this world. Cnozca didn't even notice it as it flitted about in the cave's gloom, finally alighting, as if by accident, on a spot at the back of his neck.

Cnozca jerked as it inserted a stinger, but though he wanted to slap at whatever was biting him there, he was now immobile.

The vVos sent a nerve paralyzer in through the deeply set stinger. The host would now sit quietly while the vVos went through the process of chewing an opening in the back of the neck with its mandibles. Once the creature had ingress, it dropped off its wings and legs and seated itself just beneath the skin where it could send wire-fine nerve fibers deep into the host's brain.

The sentients, gathered with so much trouble, one by one, using the orbs, were untried in the Games. They needed to be tested. All living creatures were different, and a failure on the great day of the Games was not to be tolerated. This unit had been sent out to find a host and run the necessary tests.

Cnozca sat like a statue as the vVos penetrated his brain. He was aware, but could do nothing about it. The whole possession took only about ten minutes, so skilled was the vVos in finding its way through the brains of other creatures. Sentients were, without a doubt, the most satisfying of hosts, since they were so aware. Sometimes lesser creatures, such as the black lizards that had adapted so satisfactorily to Tamir, were used in the Games because they were fast and powerful, but their brains were small and machinelike and their emotional range was very narrow—fear and rage primarily.

The vVos savored Cnozca's last efforts to fight back against what was happening to him. The human's anger was satisfying, though short-lived. When the body rose, stretched arms and legs and stepped from the cave, the vVos was in command. There was nothing unnatural about his movements, though his eyes were fixed straight ahead as he strode toward the White Grove.

Scorpio got up as he heard the flutter of wings. The flyer crept in through the entrance. There was room enough for two, though it was fairly crowded with both of them inside. The flyer had a round, soft posterior on which he could sit back and bring his handlike appendages into play. He rocked back now, and Scorpio saw that he clutched a woven sack.

Using the long-fingered "hands," the flyer opened the bag and reached in. He brought out what looked like a blue-skinned fruit of some kind and offered it to Scorpio. Scorpio realized he was hungry and accepted the offering. The tough rind resisted his efforts, so he watched the flyer create an opening with his teeth and then use his "fingers" to peel back the rind in a spiral.

Once he had imitated his host, Scorpio was able to reach the delicious blue fruit inside. It didn't taste like anything he could compare it to, but it was probably hunger that made it so delicious.

The gift of fruit made the flyer seem friendly. Of course Scorpio knew nothing about these people. Maybe feeding a captive was the prelude to some death ritual. Scorpio turned his thoughts away from that morbid scenario. Since he knew nothing of the flyer, he might as well expect the best, rather than the worst.

They exchanged names by the simple expedient of pointing to themselves and pronouncing their names slowly. The flyer was named Fz, Scorpio learned. The flyer called the fruit a *tisse*, and Scorpio thought the generic name for the flyer's species was *wefft*. Probably that could be thought of as coming a long way, but Scorpio wished for the orb, which would make all this fumbling unnecessary. He hoped, but couldn't be sure, that at some point it would return to him as it had before. In the meantime, he must do the best he could to complete his mission. The Aquay were depending on him. Soon they would be sending the ships with a thousand of their precious young and Scorpio wasn't even close to finding out what would be their fate.

After several days Scorpio had made a little more headway in learning to communicate with Fz. However he also began to feel very cramped from lack of exercise. The wefft had brought plenty of food, so he had to believe that meant Fz planned to keep him alive. When Fz returned after a foraging expedition, Scorpio pointed to his arms and legs and mimicked his stiffness. Then he used his fingers to show someone running freely.

The wefft blinked its large orange eyes. Scorpio repeated the gestures to make sure the message was getting through. At last Fz approached Scorpio and with a gesture of one of his hands indicated that Scorpio was to climb onto his back. Scorpio did so, then the wefft climbed up to the pouch opening and said a phrase that Scorpio interpreted as "Hang on!" Luckily, he did, because Fz dropped out of the pouch and let himself fall straight down. The ground was so far below, there was plenty of time for the wefft to put its powerful wings to work and pull out of the dive, but it didn't do much for Scorpio's nerves.

As they soared above the cliffs, Scorpio saw that there was another, much larger complex of webbing thrown across the canyon. There were hundreds of nest pouches dangling from it, and he saw several winged creatures similar to Fz, soaring or perched on the taut cords. As they flew near this construction, several of the weffts took flight. They gathered a moment into a spinning vortex of creatures, then shot out one by one, flying in Fz's direction.

Fz began to fly faster, but Scorpio's weight was an added burden. He couldn't outfly the pursuers. Scorpio noticed that while Fz was white-on-white, the other weffts were of brighter colors, tawny, golden, flame-orange, brown, all marked with camouflage stripes and whorls of a darker shade. As the gang of weffts approached, Scorpio became frightened. If Fz was attacked, he might well drop his burden in order to escape. He thought they had established something of a bond in their days together in the nest, but he wasn't sure he could count on it if things got dangerous.

As the weffts caught up, they began to throw small objects, screaming raucously. Scorpio felt something hit his shoulder and splatter. He was relieved to see it was only ripe fruit, not a more lethal weapon. The weffts evidently only wanted Fz to leave their territory.

After the attacking weffts had used up their arsenal, they veered off, their cries like derisive laughter. Splattered with pulp and juice, Fz kept flying.

Once it was obvious Fz was safe from further attack, he began to drop into the canyon. Scorpio heard the booming roar of fast-moving water. The tiny thread he had seen from above became the massive expanse of a turbulent brown river. Fz had evidently chosen this spot to land because his fur was matted with sticky juice and he wanted to wash. He landed on a gradual slope, moved to the river's edge, and began to splash himself, using his wings as paddles. Scorpio noted that Fz did not immerse himself completely, and decided that he was probably not a swimmer.

Luckily for me, Scorpio thought as he formulated a plan of escape. *I can't remain a prisoner and finish my mission here.* It was obvious that although Fz had treated him kindly enough, the wefft also considered him a kind of property.

After he had washed, Fz sat back to let the wind and sun dry his fur. Scorpio began to run back and forth on the riverbank, as if getting the exercise he had wanted. Noting a spot where the bank overhung the river, he began to run toward it, not slowing as he reached the edge. Behind him Fz made a hooting noise of alarm—but by then Scorpio was arching out over the water in a perfect dive.

The water was very cold, but his thick Aquay skin protected him. He swam out into the fierce current and let it take him. Aquay could stay under the water for quite a while. Fz would probably think he fell in and drowned. When at last he pushed his head above water to blow spray and grab a breath of air, he was surprised to see Fz flying over the water's surface, giving a mournful, lonely sounding call.

Scorpio floated along, watching the wefft fall farther and farther behind as its wings grew tired. The wefft gave another plaintive hoot.

Fz was evidently an outcast for some reason. Maybe it was something as simple and meaningless as his white fur. Living alone in his web, no wonder he might want some companionship, even if he had to capture it.

Scorpio began to angle toward the bank. When he pulled himself up on land, he saw Fz flying toward him with a glad cry. The creature flew erratically and looked exhausted.

I hope this isn't a mistake, Scorpio told himself. *Maybe I'll just end up as a prisoner again.*

"Strong," said Scorpio, pointing at the river as Fz landed beside him. He hoped Fz would think he had fallen in by accident and was carried off by the current. The idea of an Aquay being in danger of drowning was hilarious to Scorpio. He mimicked someone fighting the current and then laboriously climbing to safety.

Fz evidently accepted this explanation, for he only looked Scorpio over to see if he was all right, then flopped on the bank to rest.

After they had rested, they went into the forest to look for food. Fz took off and flew above the trees. A moment later Scorpio saw tree branches shaking. Fz swooped quickly and retrieved several of the fruit he had shaken loose. Scorpio picked up some from the ground. As they were eating Fz said, "All." He made an all-embracing gesture with his arms. "That falls." He made the gesture of something falling through the air. "From the sky." Here he pointed at the sky. "Is mine." He pointed to himself.

Scorpio considered the sentence. It sounded as if it might be a proverb or law of the wefft. Remembering that he had been plucked out of midair, it was little wonder that Fz had been so proprietary. Shunned by his own people, for whatever reason, he probably thought that the only way to have a companion was to own one.

"Friends," said Scorpio, hoping that was the right word. "Don't fall from the sky." He made gestures he thought appropriate with these words. Fz's crest drooped and he hooded his glowing orange eyes.

"Help me," he said. He flapped his hands to simulate flight. "Take me up." He pointed to himself. "I search."

Fz seemed to understand at least the part about taking Scorpio up, because he gestured toward his back. Scorpio climbed aboard.

Fz flew high and fast. Using this means it was easy to search more effectively. They found nothing that day, so Scorpio signaled Fz to return home.

The next day Fz ranged farther afield, beyond the mountains. Scorpio saw the deep blue surface of an ocean. Near the sea, on a long curving beach, stood a large cluster of simple, square, windowless buildings. It wasn't the city Scorpio had been looking for, but it was the first sign of technology he had yet seen on this world. There were even several structures that might be spaceship landing cradles.

He indicated to Fz that he wanted to land here, and the wefft descended. "Wait," he said to Fz, pointing toward some trees that would make good cover. The wefft flapped away, leaving Scorpio standing before a large box-like building with no ornamentation.

Chapter Eleven

Scorpio approached the door, looking about for guards. No one challenged him. He expected the door to be locked, but when he grasped the handle, it swung open.

Sudden noise nearly overwhelmed him. The vVos creatures were operating various sorts of apparatus and machinery. Scorpio wasn't sure but it looked as if they were all working on scientific experiments of some kind. The vVos workers moved unerringly and untiringly, nothing breaking their concentration on the tasks at hand. In fact, Scorpio would almost have said they moved literally as one. Humans or Aquay could not have begun to match their productivity, because individual differences would always cause delays, and human and Aquay workers needed to rest occasionally. Scorpio did not doubt that this was an efficient society, but there was also something frighteningly mechanical about it.

He watched the operation for several minutes without anyone taking any notice of him. Finally he realized he had been seen when a vVos stopped working and walked toward him. Scorpio stood his ground. "I'm the ambassador from Terrapin," he announced. "Sent by the Aquay to oversee the shipment of fry." If the vVos could send an ambassador, then perhaps this ruse would be believed and he could gather some information.

"Of course," said the vVos without missing a beat. "You are Scorpio, Liberator of the Aquay. We are pleased you have come."

Scorpio was surprised. Not only did this creature speak in the language of the Aquay, he seemed to recognize Scorpio, which was impossible. Scorpio had never seen this particular vVos before. The vVos were not wildly individual, but this one had reddish hair and a large wart on his proboscis. Their species must have a powerful news-disseminating network, he reasoned.

"I must speak with your highest ranking leader," said Scorpio.

"When you speak to one vVos, you speak to all vVos," said the creature cryptically.

"I must find out about the shipment," he went on, not sure he was up to the task of unraveling the vVos social order.

"We are pleased to report that the shipment arrived yesterday," said the vVos. "And the cargo was all in fine shape. We put the Aquay young into the Northern Sea, and they are doing quite well there. You may visit them if you like."

"Yes, I'd like that," said Scorpio. There was little he could actually do for the fry, but he could at least see if the vVos was telling the truth about their care.

The vVos conducted him out of the building by another door and led him along the beach. "You will excuse us if we do not accompany you below," it said. "Not all of us are attired for swimming."

The vVos wasn't attired at all, as far as Scorpio could see, but maybe it was a joke. He was just as glad the creature wasn't going to go into the water. Looking over the ocean's surface, he could see what he thought were several fry frisking about at some distance offshore. He slipped into the water and began to swim. The fry saw him, and quickly joined him, swimming in circles around his slow progress. An adult

Aquay could not match the speed of a fry in water, because the fry still had their swimming legs, feet with webbed toes that were angled straight back, like a fishtail. There was also a stabilizing fin between their shoulders that would be absorbed when they reached maturity.

"Do you know who I am?" he asked.

"Yes, everyone knows the Great Liberator. We were told you came ahead to make sure we would be treated well."

The group of active fry made Scorpio feel old, but it took only twelve years to reach maturity, and some of these were prepubescent, almost ready to make the land-change. He still felt a great responsibility toward them, and hoped he'd be able to think of something to get them back to Terrapin.

The youngsters dived and Scorpio followed them, though he could not stay down as long as they could. As they neared the bottom, Scorpio saw a huge pale pink shell mottled with amber. When he pointed to it, one of the fry said, "That's a torata. Don't get too close. They can be dangerous if they're disturbed."

Scorpio swam no nearer, but as he watched, he saw three fry coming from another direction. They swam purposefully, with eyes fixed straight ahead. They each carried tridents in their small hands. The fry with Scorpio began to yell warnings to the others, but their words were unheeded.

The three circled the shell, yelling a challenge. "Come out, Old Oyster, come out and fight!" One of them used the trident to smack the side of the shell. Several tentacles studded with sucker disks burst from beneath the shell. A tentacle wrapped about one fry, who jerked and twitched as the sucker disks attached to his skin. One of the other fry used his trident to stab the tentacle, which writhed like a wounded worm, driving the attacker away.

"Those fry are acting strangely," said Scorpio. "The Aquay are a timid race. Why should they be so aggressive?"

"I don't know," said a fry beside Scorpio. "One of them is Kivi, a friend of mine. I didn't think he'd do anything like this."

"Maybe when they see the torata fighting back, they'll retreat," said Scorpio, but the fry didn't seem to be calling off their attack, even though one of them was now held limply in a tentacle's coils. The other two swam in from different directions, jabbing their tridents at a spot toward the bottom of the shell. Suddenly a spray of inky water was expelled from the shell, darkening the water.

Scorpio swam closer, trying to see what was happening through the ink. He wondered if he should join the fight in order to rescue the fry, though he had to admit that the fry were the aggressors, since the torata hadn't been bothering anyone. When he got close enough, he saw one of the fry grasped in a dark beak that jutted from inside the circle of tentacles. Even though he was cut almost in two, the fry was still fighting, driving his trident into one of the torata's large yellow eyes. The only fry left swimming was not running away, as might be expected, but instead closed in. As the torata thrashed, a trident buried deep in his eye, his beak closed completely, cutting the captured fry in two, the parts of the body dropping to the sea floor. The last fry stuck his trident into the thing's other eye, just as ropy tentacles reached up to grasp him. The fry was quickly crushed, but another gout of ink was released into the water and Scorpio could see no more, though he could hear the terrible thrashing of the blinded monster. Abruptly the sounds of struggle stopped. Scorpio supposed that one of the tridents had penetrated deeply enough to kill the torata.

"Let's get out of here," suggested one of the fry with Scorpio. Scorpio swam sluggishly toward the surface. He had almost forgotten that he had to breathe.

The fight had been over so quickly, there had been no time to try to separate the combatants.

"Kivi was my friend," one of the fry was saying, "but there was something wrong with him. He was acting crazy."

"I don't know what's going on," Scorpio said as they broke the surface, "but I'm going to try to find out."

The fight had left him numb. This would not have happened on Terrapin, but they weren't on Terrapin. He had to question the vVos about what had happened to these fry since they had been brought here.

He walked from the ocean, waving to the fry, who returned the gesture and dived beneath the waves.

A unit flew into the cluster and joined the communal brain. It bore a message: "Scorpio, the Liberator of Terrapin, has arrived on Tamir."

Instantaneously, information was passed, causing an ebb and flow of questions, answers and speculations as the vVos considered the problem.

We knew he probably had captured the orbs we gave to the Hunters. By now the three may well have combined, judging by what our own orbs are doing. Ever since we discovered the orbs during a the faster-than-light experiment, they have been something of an enigma. The orbs certainly took the place of the faster-than-light craft we could never successfully develop. And we also discovered they travel through time, though this was a mere novelty, since a being such as a vVos that has always been and always will be has little interest in traveling through time. Also orbs are limited in being able to carry but one or two at a time. Scorpio could bring an army one at a time. It would be quite obvious if that were happening; our units would be reporting it and no such reports have arrived. Well, then Scorpio is most likely alone. Can one mortal creature do us harm? Where is he now? Under the sea with his Aquay young. Did you not know we are running a test of the undersea equipment today? No, we did not have that information, having been at the laboratory complex for some time. But what's the harm if Scorpio does see the experiment? He can have no idea of its significance. And even if he is suspicious he will be dead soon. We will kill him then? Of course. It is necessary and will add to our enjoyment.

When Scorpio returned to the labs, his anger had cooled. There were a lot more of the vVos than there were of him, so charging in with accusations wasn't a good idea.

"We hope you were satisfied with the condition of the fry," said a vVos who resembled but didn't appear to be the one he had talked to before.

"Yes, they were in good health. But I'm puzzled. While I was below I saw a fight between three fry and a shelled creature called a torata."

"Is that so strange? Surely, there is conflict on your own world."

"I can't say that the Aquay exist in total peace," said Scorpio, "but we are a gentle people, usually. This was a bloody fight to the death, with all three fry killed. I couldn't see that the torata did anything to provoke them. It was only sitting on the sea floor when they attacked it."

"If you think this strange we can certainly investigate the incident for you," said the vVos agreeably.

Scorpio felt his suspicions rise. The vVos had never tried to placate anyone before. On Terrapin the the vVos ambassador had been quite arrogant, demanding the shipment of fry.

"You requested before to meet with our highest ranking leader. We have decided to honor your request. This way, please."

Scorpio followed, thinking he must be alert for an attack. He was shown into a small room crowded with shelves laden with laboratory equipment and other less identifiable artifacts. It looked like a storage room, though a chair had been placed in the center of it. The vVos gestured for him to sit.

"Our representative will be in shortly," said the vVos as it shut the door and left.

Scorpio jumped to his feet and tried the door. It was unlocked. Still, he had the feeling he was being set up. He had to be ready for action whenever the attack came.

After he had sat there on the alert for quite a while, with nothing happening, his suspicions became dulled. The room was close and musty-smelling. A mothlike insect with blue-edged wings flew through shafts of dusty sunlight. He knew it was stupid, but he had always had an irrational fear of flying insects. Even the sight of one made him feel as if insect legs were crawling on his body. He was usually able to suppress the fear as he reached adulthood, but it made him more aware of winged insects than others were.

He felt himself about to doze off.

Chapter Twelve

Before Scorpio could fall asleep, he felt the back of his neck brushed by fluttering wings and reached back quickly.

"Ah-ha!" he said, bringing his hand around and using his other hand to create a cage. The insect batted its wings desperately against his fingers. Watching it gave Scorpio a queasy feeling and his first impulse was to crush it, but he told himself such a thing was harmless and he shouldn't let his silly fears rule his actions.

He went to the one narrow window, opened it and set the insect free outside. As he closed the window, the insect fluttered against the glass tenaciously. "Go pollinate a flower," he told it.

His thoughts turned away from the pesky insect and back to his vigil. No leader of the vVos had arrived and perhaps none was going to. He didn't know what purpose it served to have him sitting here, but he wasn't going to take this treatment.

He peeked out into the corridor. It was empty. He stepped out and began to walk purposefully toward the outer door, staring straight ahead in his concentration.

Before he could get there, two vVos came from another doorway. Scorpio was deciding to run when one of them gave him a jaunty wave that could only be a friendly salute.

"See you in the cluster," said the other.

Scorpio returned the wave and continued his progress toward the door. Breaking into a run when he was outside, he approached the trees, calling for Fz.

The wefft wasn't under the trees or in them. He supposed the bond between himself and Fz was not yet so strong that it would wait for him all this time. Behind him he began to hear excited shouts. The vVos must have discovered his escape by now and were organizing pursuit. They were slow-moving, but he was outnumbered. In his predicament he hardly noticed the gray-winged insect exactly like the one he'd freed fly into the clearing where he stood. It hovered for a moment over his head. He was aware of it, but his attention was diverted by thoughts of being recaptured.

As he was about to run farther into the forest to escape pursuit, he caught sight of a golden gleam hovering in midair. As he watched, it became a sphere and settled gracefully to the ground at his feet. The orb had returned. He had never been so glad to see anything in his life.

It was very large compared to the earlier orb he had used, but he knew that after a combining, the orb grew larger and glowed with a brighter light. He had considered the orbs to be mating, but instead of reproducing their kind, they were dwindling in number. However, at the moment he wasn't of a mind to question the thing.

The insect above his head dived.

So eager was he to grab up the orb that when the insect alit on his neck this time, he swatted at it reflexively, broke the delicate wings and crushed the protective casing.

The unit fell unheeded onto the forest floor, as Scorpio grasped the orb and jumped. Under normal circumstances, the unit could extrude new wings, but this one had been irreparably damaged by Scorpio's blow. In this way at least one small part of the vVos was vulnerable, though the vVos would miss this part as much as a human would miss a fingernail paring. The legs were undamaged. It hoisted itself to its feet and began to creep over forest debris. Some of the brain matter was still operative, but it was muddled and confused. Its last order circled in its fibers. "Possess a body." However, it no longer knew exactly which body was to be possessed, and without wings, such an order would be difficult to carry out. Still, it was nothing but a biological machine and knew nothing of the odds against it. It continued to walk, searching.

The orb obeyed Scorpio's command to jump into orb space, but it didn't bring him instantaneously to the spot where he had left Leah, as he had commanded. He hovered in orb space and pictures began to form in his mind.

He saw a strange forest, or he supposed that was what it was. The trees and bushes were crystalline, glowing prismatically like foliage after an ice storm, and when the wind blew there was a cool tinkling sound like the ringing of wind chimes. It was a lonely, otherworldly sound.

Scorpio didn't have a clear view of the scene because when he tried to look at things directly, they blurred, so he had to be satisfied with peripheral vision. He got the idea that the crystalline forest did not grow on Tamir or on any world he could get to.

Hanging from the branches above were orbs, like this one, but there were an unimaginable number of them, like ripe fruit, each one giving off a contented golden glow. This was what caused the prismatic effect on the crystalline trees.

As Scorpio watched, an elliptical metal craft began to form. It didn't land, as such, it simply became real, detail by detail. The pattern of the rivets came first and then the outline of the hull. When it had fully appeared, he saw that the hull was blackened and smoking. He supposed that was because of coming through some unimaginable barrier of time and space.

When the circular door opened, Scorpio was surprised to see several vVos emerge. Their hairy ugliness was accentuated here, but they walked about, gawking and gesticulating in wonderment. Scorpio felt himself become angry when they clambered about in the delicate forest, shattering exquisite glassy formations. They put bits of this destruction in plastic bags, as if for future study. Then boosting each other up, they began to pick the orbs. Scorpio couldn't be sure how many were gathered before noticing that the hull of their craft had begun to blister and smoke, as if things of metal had a difficult time existing here. Quickly, the vVos got back into their craft, and detail by detail, it disappeared again. Scorpio supposed that one voyage into this dimension was all the battered craft could sustain.

The vision faded and Scorpio found himself in the spot where he had left Leah, the orb lying obediently at his feet. "Thanks for telling me that," he said aloud. "Somehow I always knew you could communicate, if we could only find a way. Combining must have made you more powerful." Scorpio had the feeling that the orb could tell him much more, and he was eager to know, but a headache pounded his temples from the contact. He could only stand so much of this direct communication from the powerful organism the orb had become.

Fz had waited for Scorpio for some time, but Scorpio didn't return from the boxlike structure. Fz was beginning to get the feeling he had been tricked before when Scorpio told him the current had carried him away. Fz had seen the Aquay's graceful dive. He had only pretended to believe what Scorpio said, so that he could keep his illusion of having a friend. Now that Scorpio went inside and hadn't come out, he began to think that the Aquay was making fun of him by leaving him waiting out here indefinitely. After his expulsion from wefft society, he was more than a little paranoid.

Fz was a ghostwefft, an albino. His kind had been sent into exile throughout the existence of wefft society because of their strange appearance and a color that was considered in some way "evil." Fz knew that this was not the natural home of the wefft race. According to the communal tales he had heard as a child, weffts had been brought by the Spirit of Flight to this new world to thrive and multiply, which they had done. But even in a new world the old laws applied. Fz was exiled after his fifth year, when he had some realistic chance of surviving on his own. This was progress of a sort because the tales told of ghostwefft infants being left to starve.

Fz had not starved, except in spirit. When he had plucked Scorpio out of the sky, he thought a whole new life was going to open up for him. No more solitary existence. *So much for a new world and a new life,* he thought sourly.

Winging back toward his web, he couldn't resist flying near the wefft colony. He knew he would be chased away, but he still couldn't keep himself from wanting a glimpse of his own kind. As he flew closer, he realized that no one was coming up to chase him. Something was happening in the web below that had gotten almost everyone's attention. A horde of wefft had gathered, clinging to the cords until they sagged under the weight of so many bodies. A little above this crowd two wefft soared. As Fz hovered there a moment, he realized that they were doing more than just flying.

One wefft, a large tiger-striped orange female, veered close to the other, a brindle, swinging a heavy wing joint toward his head. The brindle dodged at the last minute, then flew above the tiger-stripe, trying to force her down. Tiger-stripe did lose some altitude, bouncing off one of the web's cords, which shook the entire web. Several observers were nearly unseated.

Though flying slowly and taking advantage of wind currents to hover, Fz had to bank and return to see the rest of the combat. He was surprised to see this. The communal tales told of feuds and even wefft wars in the past, but the race had mellowed. Disputes were sent to the Council of Ten. The wefft had lived in peace for generations on their own world. He wondered what was so different about this planet that made one wefft turn viciously upon another.

Of course he hadn't forgotten that they had turned viciously enough on him, but they only used fruit or dirt clods as weapons. If they had really meant to hurt him, they could easily have done so.

If he had had any illusions that this was only a flying match or a mock combat, they were shattered when he saw the tiger fly near the brindle and slash him with the curved knife used for cord-cutting. Blood poured down the brindle's side and he flew erratically for a moment. Fz saw that the brindle was also armed with a knife, when he wheeled back and cut a long gash in the tiger's left wing. Tiger was then in trouble, and she began to fall, but the brindle didn't just let her go, he followed, and the two of them grappled in midair, screeching and pulling out tufts of fur, which floated behind them as they fell. Their cries grew faint with distance and then both of them were lost in the green blur of foliage below.

Fz did not see how either would have survived such a fall. The brindle might have only hovered and watched his enemy die, but he almost seemed to want to die with her.

A few wefft on the cords below looked up and saw Fz. He was afraid they would give chase, so he wheeled away. However, the violence must have stunned them because no one gave chase.

Fz was ashamed at what he had seen. He wasn't an official part of the wefft race, but he had always believed in certain standards. The two must have been renegades, fighting over some dispute. Nothing else made any sense.

Chapter Thirteen

The vVos unit that Scorpio had crushed continued to walk through the forest. It was little more than a set of legs carrying puzzled brain matter in a broken casing. It was important to find a body and possess it, that was the first thing. Another desire underlay that, but it was vague.

It moved inexorably toward the mountain range, having no idea of the barriers that stood in its way.

Leah sat in the grove, watching the barbaric men eat and drink. Their appetites were prodigious. They did this every day, singing and jesting, as if it were their sole purpose in life. However, Leah noticed that one of them sat at a little distance from the others and on this day did not join in their feasting and song. He looked somber, staring straight ahead, even though his companions often said something to him in a jesting manner. One even tried to pull him closer to the group, but he simply shrugged his friend off.

Perhaps he is ill, Leah thought. She felt a certain amount of lassitude herself. There was little she could do but eat and drink and observe the other Earth people. Occasionally, she saw Roland, who pretended that she wasn't there. She had begun to concentrate on Scorpio on the off chance that their mental contact would reassert itself, but so far nothing had happened.

As Leah sat there, toying with her food, Hatshepsut came running toward her, jabbering about something. They had managed to exchange a few phrases of each other's languages, but now Hatshepsut was so excited, she fairly babbled and Leah could not get her to slow down so she could find out what was wrong. The reason for her excitement came striding into the grove.

"The madman," said Leah. "He's back. No wonder you were so upset." It was indeed the man who had attacked Hatshepsut and Leah earlier. His feather cloak looked the worse for wear, but he still carried the stone knife in his belt.

"The vVos won't let him harm anyone here," said Leah to Hatshepsut, but the madman looked even madder than usual, with his eyes staring. He walked purposefully into the grove, drawing the black knife. Surprisingly, the morose member of the barbarian's party got to his feet, placed his horned helmet on his head, picked up his round shield and drew the ax that was hanging from his belt. His companions acted surprised at his actions, and two of them rushed forward to try to stop him, but he brushed them off, more violently than before, saying a guttural word that was almost certainly a curse.

"The vVos won't permit any violence," said Leah, looking around to see if any of the vVosian guards were about. She saw two of them taking their ease beneath a tree. They almost certainly saw what was about to happen, but they didn't act.

Cnozca leapt forward with a roar of rage, slashing wildly with the dagger. Its edge caught on the shield and drew a jagged line across the hardened leather. He of the horned helmet swung the ax, but it missed and slammed into one of the white trees. It seemed to Leah that there was something infinitesimally off about their movements, as if they weren't quite familiar with these weapons.

Cnozca pressed forward as if he felt himself invulnerable and drove his dagger beneath the shield into the man's thigh.

The barbarian screamed as the sharp blade penetrated, and blood spurted. Cnozca jumped back in time to avoid the swing of the ax. It looked inaccurate anyway due to the pain of the barbarian's wound.

They circled each other, and this time the barbarian's ax was swung more accurately. The blunt end hit Cnozca in the ribs and threw him off his feet. He had to scramble madly to avoid the next blow, but by inches he did it.

By now everyone in the grove had gathered to watch. "Isn't anyone going to try to stop this?" asked Leah, but she said it for herself, since most of them wouldn't understand her, and it didn't seem a good idea, even to her, for someone to try to get between the combatants. Their eyes were locked on each other, and neither showed any signs of wanting to run. The wounds they had given each other must have caused great pain, but both moved like fighting automatons, pain forgotten in the heat of battle.

From inside Cnozca (and also his enemy), the vVos reveled in the effects of the combat. Cnozca was still aware enough to feel the pain and experience the horror of the situation, even though he had little control of the body itself. The vVos experienced his emotions in full and savored them, as a connoisseur savored fine wine, but he still anticipated the thrill of the ultimate sensation.

Using the Aztec's wiry, muscular body and lack of encumbering equipment and clothing as an advantage, the unit inside Cnozca moved quickly in and out of range, slashing with the knife. Ordinarily, a man without the heavy weapons of his opponent would be at a disadvantage because he would fear being struck, but the vVos suppressed Cnozca's natural instincts. Because the body was expendable, it could take a certain number of blows, if they weren't direct ones, that crushed a skull, or sheared away an arm or leg. Direct, personal combat was also a specialty of the vVos because there was little satisfaction in sitting in a machine and blowing one's enemy up, if the experience of combat was the important thing. That was why few soldiers of a technological age had been chosen. In the vVos's opinion, they weren't useful. The Norseman wasn't exactly technologically oriented with his crude shield and battle-ax, and yet the techniques of using these were more difficult for the unit to master.

The Cnozca body circled and moved in quickly again, just as the Norseman began to swing the ax. Cnozca drove the dagger into the Norseman's throat from the side, and stepped back, right into the path of the ax blow. A solid strike shattered his rib cage, sharp bones piercing his heart. Both tottered about for a few minutes, and then fell. As Cnozca's blood trickled out into the dirt, so did his life, and this was what the vVos had been waiting for.

Death poured into all the vVos's receptors in an unending wave. There was the gush of powerful hormones throughout the body, as it fought its last struggle for survival. The vVos imbibed it like a drug, experiencing it to the full. Currents in the brain circled hopelessly, snippets of the being's life coming to the fore, fading out again, as in troubled dreams. Hope of an extended existence created the fleeting hallucination of traveling down a tunnel toward a distant light, greeting loved ones, old friends. But now all striving began to fade as systems shut down, one by one.

The vVos battened on death, grew giddy on it. A being who had always been and always would be found temporary excitement in the experience; the vVos could live its predictable life, allaying its curiosity about the universe by carrying on scientific experiments and exploration for a thousand years, but after the millennium it needed its fix of death.

The vVos unit in the Cnozca body would return to the cluster, as would the one that had inhabited the Norseman. There it would share its experiences and the cluster would seethe with dreams, but this was only a tiny foretaste of what the Games held in store.

When the cluster reached a critical mass of anticipation, almost every section of the brain would outfit itself with wings and legs and possess a body. Then the carnage would begin. On land, on sea and in the air, beings would lock in mortal combat. The vVos would gorge itself on the excitement of death.

In the aftermath, the survivors, if there were any, would continue to live here, and if the vVos were lucky, they would breed, rebuilding the population for the advent of the next round of Games. Unfortunately the vVos had often, in their enthusiasm, practically denuded the planet of life, which was why they had to bring so many new life-forms here.

The vVos would gather in its cluster, sharing a surfeit of death, content to suffer whatever hangover it might feel afterward. Then it would settle in for another thousand years of uneventful life. It had always been so, and always would be.

In the aftermath of the fight, the humans stood around talking softly. The Norsemen had gathered around their fallen comrade. In the midst of this solemn scene, the orb bubble began to form with Scorpio in its heart. It was a strange occurrence from the humans' viewpoint, but what they had just seen had sobered them. In this new world, they were probably also becoming a little tired of wonders, so a gray-skinned alien alighting from a bubble-craft made hardly a ripple in their composure.

"Scorpio, I'd almost given you up," said Leah, running up to him.

"It took me some time to find you," said Scorpio. "Step inside the orb with me and we'll commune and share our experiences. It'll save a lot of telling."

Leah took Scorpio's hand and he activated the orb. In the timelessness of orb space their minds connected and their experiences mingled. When they snapped out of orb space again, Leah said, "Your experience with the fry. The same thing happened here. These two men just fought to the death."

"And of course they were peace-loving folk to begin with," said Scorpio innocently.

"Well, not exactly," said Leah, "but before the vVos enforced peace in this grove. Suddenly these two men were allowed to fight to the death."

"Perhaps the vVos can release a chemical to make beings more warlike," said Scorpio, "but what purpose would it serve?"

"I know none of this makes sense now," said Leah, "but I have a feeling we need to find out as soon as we can."

A side effect of being in orb space was that now Leah could understand the languages of the folk in the grove. She wasn't sure how all the knowledge had been provided so quickly and without exploding her head. She heard the Norsemen talking as they gathered about their companion.

"Eric, you told us this was Valhalla," said a scarred man with a rusty-red beard. "Where we would eat and drink and enjoy ourselves for eternity. If we are already dead, how can my brother Lars die?"

"When I saw the feasting was never-ending here, it was the logical thing to think. Besides, perhaps war still continues, even in Valhalla."

"Wherever this may be, we must honor the dead," said another. They began wandering around the grove, gathering armloads of fallen branches, which they brought back to stack in a huge pile. When they had finished, they lifted the corpse atop it and someone struck a spark. Fire climbed swiftly through the dead wood.

"Something must also be done with the body of the other," said Hatshepsut.

"We don't know what his burial customs were," said Leah. Hatshepsut looked surprised to hear Leah speaking Egyptian, then seemed to accept it as another wonder of the place. "You are charitable, since this is the man who almost killed you."

"I don't do it out of charity," said Hatshepsut. "Everyone knows that the *ka* must be shown the way through Anubis' gate through ritual and proper burial. Otherwise it might roam about, harassing the living."

"I'm sure that's true in your country," said Leah diplomatically, "but I don't think we have much to fear from the wandering dead in this land. Still, we'll have to make some arrangements. Perhaps the barbaric men would help us prepare a pyre."

"Destroy the body? Never! It is a necessity in the afterlife. There are lots of caves in the hills, perhaps one of them would make a proper tomb if we sealed the entrance with some stones."

The idea of burning Cnozca's body was so shocking to Hatshepsut that Leah humored her. She circled among the others in the grove, using her new language skills to recruit a burial party. They soon found a small cave and with some effort were able to seal the entrance with a pile of stones. Hatshepsut even said a short prayer, though Leah had the feeling it was more to keep Cnozca in the tomb than out of any sympathy for him. They returned, feeling they had done the best they could, and with those grim chores out of the way, they could make plans to use the orb to return everyone to his or her own time.

Chapter Fourteen

As Leah and Scorpio returned to the grove, they saw a golden bubble pop into existence, and inside it was the ugly, hairy shape of a vVos. The vVos still had orbs themselves, and they had evidently used theirs to track Scorpio here.

"We'd better jump," said Scorpio, holding the orb out to Leah, but intense rainbow light began to radiate from the orb and it would not obey Scorpio's command.

The vVos's orb was now behaving similarly. It was all the creature could do to hold on to it.

"They're trying to combine again," shouted Scorpio.

"Don't let it go!" replied Leah. "It's our only way home!"

Scorpio tried, but the orb melted through his fingers and bounced onto the ground. The other orb did the same, and the two rolled together rapidly. An explosion of light made the humans in the vicinity jump for cover, but Leah knew there was no danger. However, since the orb was gone again, they were on their own.

"I hate it when that happens!" said Scorpio.

The vVos who had ridden in on the orb was stumbling about blindly. Leah asked the Norsemen to take charge of him and not let him escape. The Vikings acted confused about the situation, but seemed glad that there was an opportunity to do something other than eat bland porridge. They hustled the vVos off to his captivity.

"What can we do now?" asked Scorpio. "We're right back where we started."

"Not exactly," said Leah. "I can now communicate with the Earth folk, and they've been here just long enough to want to escape, I think. Someone just has to show them the way."

"What way? What sort of action makes sense in this situation?"

"The lab complex sounds as if it might be the central headquarters for the vVos," said Leah. "If we could capture it, perhaps we could find records and learn why we were all brought here."

"You're forgetting," said Scorpio, "that humans can't pass through the fear-borders created by the vVos.

"There must be a way," said Leah. "They're only devices, not magic. I have an idea."

Leah walked into the deepest part of the forest. She could see nothing above in the deeply shadowed tree canopy, yet she felt that she was being watched.

"Tree people!" she called out.

There was a rustling in the leaves above and a simian face looked through a gap in the foliage. She had spoken in the strange chirping language of the hominids. Her use of their words caused a certain amount of confusion among the trees. She saw branches sway, leaves fall as the hominids moved among them, still keeping themselves invisible.

"You of the sharp eyes, chattering tongues, come down and talk with your cousin. I can't hurt you."

A male swung down from the branches above, landing agilely beside her. A female joined him, and then a younger female. They were wary at first, but then were examining Leah more closely, which consisted of picking at her clothing and hair with their crooked fingers. Up close, they had a musky animal smell, but Leah retained her composure. She needed their help.

When they were assured that she meant no harm and was in some way similar to them, she said, "I'm looking for some small objects, hidden in the trees. I'll show you the place."

"We see everything in the trees," said the male boastfully, hammering on his chest. "Nothing gets by us."

Leah and the hominids approached the barrier. "That is the scary place," said the youngest female. "No one ever goes there."

"It's a scary place for me, too," said Leah, "and you don't need to cross the line. Just try to control your fear a little and approach it closely through the treetops. You should see a small box or something similar. It is a box full of fear."

"We will try," said the male, catching hold of a low-hanging branch and swinging up. The females followed, and for a while Leah saw nothing of them, then she heard their high-pitched chittering voices.

"There it is!" they said, repeating the words over and over. Leah saw them capering through the treetops, and it was a while before she could get them to subdue their excitement and actually point out the objects they had seen in the trees.

One of the females stretched out on a branch and pointed upward. Leah could see the edge of some sort of box or case fastened to a branch. The male chittered even louder and jumped about as he pointed. It was quite a while before Leah saw the box he had discovered. She supposed they were similar to the devices used in the grove to frighten the humans into submission.

"We are the finest people," said the adult female in a rusty-gate screech. "We have found the box of fear."

"What good does that do?" asked the younger female. "It's still too scary to go near. It scares me even from here."

"That's all right," Leah yelled up to them. "You've done enough. I'll handle it from here."

She returned to the grove and approached the man in fringed leather and animal-tail cap. "We need your help," she told him. "These creatures who are feeding us are holding us prisoner here."

"Well, I know that, little lady," said the frontiersman. "Every time I went out to explore, I couldn't go no farther because something just took the heart right out of me. But what can an ignorant backwoodsman like old Jed do about it?"

"I've noticed your weapon," she said, indicating the tall rifle at his side.

Proud of the gun, he held it out for her inspection. As projectile weapons went, it looked pretty primitive. She had watched him use it, and there were several steps before it could even be fired. He had to stuff something in the barrel and pour in some substance he kept in a cow's horn hanging at his belt. Since he had fired it a number of times, she wasn't even sure he had much of the substance left.

"Well, I can hit the eye of a squirrel at thirty paces," said Jed. "A course, there ain't any squirrels here."

"I didn't have squirrels in mind," said Leah. "Come with me."

As Leah and Scorpio watched, Jed went through the complicated ritual of loading the rifle. Leah pointed up into the trees, indicating the first of the boxes the hominids had found. Jed stuck his thumb in his mouth and held it up, and Leah thought this must be some strange religious ritual until she decided that maybe he was only finding out from what direction the wind was blowing. Then he spat out a wad of leaves. She noticed that he had the rather disgusting habit of chewing the leaves of a common bush. Then he cuddled the rifle next to his cheek. "Better hope I loaded 'er right or I'll blow my own ear off," he joked. The gun went off with what seemed a tremendous explosion in the quiet clearing and Leah and Scorpio cheered as the box flew into a thousand shards.

"Now the other one," said Leah eagerly.

"Can't fire more than one shot at a time," said Jeb laconically. "Got to recharge 'er."

On the second shot the last box was blasted out of the tree.

"Will that do it?" asked Scorpio.

"I don't know," said Leah. "It's possible the hominids didn't find all the boxes. I guess I'll try." Reluctantly, she began to walk toward the wall of trees that had once been an impenetrable barrier for her kind. She expected at any moment to be struck by a wave of fear, but she kept walking and nothing happened.

"All clear!" she shouted, and Jed came to join her.

"Durned if you didn't do it, little lady. Now we can get out of this jail. Only, when we do get out, where are we going to go? I can't get back to Kaintuck from here, can I?"

"No, I'm afraid you can't, at least not now," said Leah. "But I have a plan that might help us figure out why we're here and what can be done about it."

"If you have a plan, little lady, you're the only one I've met here who does. That's good enough for old Jed."

It was growing late, so Leah and Scorpio gathered wood for a campfire and Jed went into the woods to see what he could flush out. Leah heard the report of the rifle and a little later Jed returned carrying a small animal with a blue and gray spotted pelt. Soon it was cleaned and roasting over the fire.

"I don't suppose you've ever been to Kaintuck," said Jed. "I miss it somethin' awful. It was plumb orneriness that got me here." Leah and Scorpio listened as he told his story, staring drowsily into the fire.

Jed had been at Churchy LeBec's Trading Post. Churchy was called that because he was always smacking his lips and saying "*Cherchez la femme*." Churchy's was the only trace of civilization for a hundred miles, so most of the backwoodsmen gathered there when they could.

Jed had just traded in a stack of prime beaver pelts and he'd used part of the money to buy some whiskey. He'd just been sitting there idling away the time and would probably have been there still if Angel Hennessy hadn't swaggered in. He was called that because he wasn't one, obviously.

As was the way of things in those parts, Angel and Jed began to compare notes, not exactly quietly. "I'm the best hunter, the best trapper, the best tracker, the best storyteller this side of the Mississip, bar none!" Angel had boasted at the top of his lungs.

"Yeah, I've trapped more beaver and muskrat, brought down more ducks, kilt more bears and faced down more catamounts than you've got teeth in your head!" By this time the loungers at Churchy's had all gathered around to see what would come of this.

Both Angel and Jed had gotten to their none-too-unsteady feet at this point and were circling around each other, acting as if they were trying for wrestling holds. But the only weapons they wanted to use so far were words.

"I can outjump, outholler, outspit, outrun and outtalk you!" yelled Angel, turning red in the face.

"I'm a ring-tailed, silver-dollar wonder of the world," said Jed. "I can do anything I say I can. I'll take any bet, any dare, and do it twice on Sunday just to make you look bad."

"Any bet, any dare?" asked Angel. "That's a laugh!"

"Take me up on it, tinhorn. I'm just itchin' to show you up in front of all these folks."

"You know Old Honeypaw, the grizzly bear?"

"Who in these parts don't?"

"Can you bring in his hide?"

"Betcher boots."

Jed stopped, shook his head and staggered about. He shouldn't have drunk so much of that rye whiskey. It was making him crazy.

"Told you he was just a bag of hot air," said Angel.

Jed saw the looks on the faces of the other trappers and hunters. Old Honeypaw had accounted for his share of mauled hunters. Some of them had died.

"Aw, I was only funnin'," said Angel innocently. "You don't want to go after that old bear."

Jed looked around the circle of men. It was too late; the damage had been done. If he didn't at least have a try at it, he'd get a new name for sure, "Yella Jed." Names had a way of sticking in these parts.

"Well, hell, I've been wantin', a bear rug," said Jed. "A *big* rug! 'Bout the size of Old Honeypaw. It's near spring, time for the bears to come roarin' out of their caves, lean and hungry. Reckon I'll start layin' for Old Honeypaw right away."

It took Jed over a week to begin looking for Honeypaw, but when he felt he couldn't hold out any longer, he shouldered his rifle, put his knife in its scabbard and set out.

There never was a place like the Kentucky back-woods in the spring he thought. The streams rushing bank full, the forest teeming with game, the kind of riches that just don't run out. But then he heard the hollow roaring of a grizzly bear just awakening after the long sleep with an empty belly and wished he was anyplace but there. Slipping through the trees, he spied on the grizzly as it reared up against a tree and left its mark high on its trunk with its immense claws. Big, but not big enough. Not Old Honeypaw.

He searched for hours and felt he wasn't going to have any success when he saw a bear fishing in the shallows of a stream. This bear had great humped shoulders with silver-speckled fur, paws as big as dinner plates, and when he roared upon missing a good catch, the treetops trembled.

So did Jed. To face such a monster as this had to be the height of folly, but a man will do many things to keep a good name. With unsteady hands that spilled black powder all around, Jed loaded his rifle.

When he had finished, Old Honeypaw was lumbering onto the bank of the stream, his nostrils quivering as the wind blew Jed's scent to him. Jed was as ready as he'd ever be when Honeypaw bellowed and charged. The gun went off with a puff of smoke that blinded Jed for an instant.

When he could see again what he saw was a bear rearing up seemingly house-top high and ready to crush him with its massive forelegs. Jed backpedaled quickly, dodged aside and began to run toward the nearest tree. He shinnied up it like a monkey and clung there, looking down and feeling safe.

That was until Old Honeypaw began to shinny up the tree himself. Unfortunately, the slender tree wasn't stout enough to bear the bruin's weight, and as Honeypaw climbed, the tree bent farther and farther until Jed's tree-top had almost reached the ground.

Jed stepped out of the treetop onto solid ground and looked around for a safer haven. He was making for a cleft in the rocks when he realized that he and the bear and the landscape were bathed in a golden light.

Over his head a golden sphere hovered. Jed was a plain man; there wasn't room in his world for the inexplicable, so as the sphere dropped, he began to run again. So did Old Honeypaw and when the bubble reached the ground, it closed around the bear and began to rise again.

Jed watched dumbfounded. At first glance it looked like there were two bears in there, a little one and a big one, and then Old Honeypaw bellied out the side of the bubble with a swipe of his huge paw. Jed could see the outline of the claws, but whatever the bubble was made out of, it wasn't soap because it didn't break.

The orb descended hastily and expelled the bear, who reared up, clawing as the bubble rose out of its reach.

By this time Jed had reached the narrow cleft in the rocks and began to push himself inside. He almost fit. Only his feet were left out. Feet were about the size of a bear's breakfast, he opined, and he desperately scrambled to bring all of himself inside.

The golden orb, instead of giving up, was flying his way. It settled quietly over his feet and the bearlike thing inside grabbed him and began to pull him slowly into the orb.

"And that," Jed said to Leah and Scorpio, "is how I come to be here. And it's mostly the truth, with only enough lies to make it interesting."

Chapter Fifteen

Leah's next step was to communicate with as many of the other prisoners as possible and talk them into coming with her. They needed an impressive army if they were to capture the lab complex. She realized that she was the only one who could mobilize the humans, since they were so isolated from each other by their different cultures and languages. Even with that advantage, she still had to convince them that there was danger on their world, and since she didn't know exactly what the danger was, that might be difficult. She only knew she had the feeling that time was running out and they had to do something.

Leah approached the camp cautiously because she wasn't familiar with the people who had established it. As far as she knew they had always kept to themselves, not taking advantage of the grove. The lean-to was sturdy and well reinforced with branches. A stream ran nearby giving the camp a fresh water supply. If they could find edibles or kill game, it was probably possible to survive well here, which was probably why they hadn't ever come to the grove. A plume of smoke rose from a fire of green wood, which could not serve for cooking, so must have had some other purpose, though Leah could not guess what it was.

Two people crouching in the lean-to came out as Leah approached. One was a tall woman with short, curly hair, wearing a leather jacket and cloth trousers; the other was a stocky man of middle years. They seemed nervous to see Leah, so she tried to seem as peaceful as possible.

When Leah got close enough, she saw that the woman carried a revolver. Leah's travels into the twentieth century made her aware of the efficiency of these projectile weapons. Leah chose her words carefully as she explained to the woman what had happened and where she was.

"She's crazy," said the man as Leah finished. "We've got to stay here, keep our signal fire going. You know that people are out searching for us since we didn't reach Howland Island."

"Fred, we've explored quite a ways and never found the ocean, so we're not on an island. We never found the wreckage of the Lockheed, either. I don't like the idea of flying saucers any better than you do, but I don't think we're on Earth anymore."

The man sighed, his shoulders drooping. "I'll put out the signal fire."

When the woman explained how they'd gotten there, Leah took the book from her belt pouch.

"I think this belongs to you," she said.

• • •

Leah found Roland by the pool where they had first met. She had talked to everyone else first, not wanting to have to face him. She hadn't spoken to him since their last meeting, and each had tried to pretend the other wasn't there.

"I need your help," she said.

"That sounds familiar," said Roland. "Will you lead me another chase after a damsel in distress?"

"It's really everyone who needs your help," said Leah. "All the Earth folk. We've decided to attack the vVos stronghold and find information as to why we're all here. We might even be able to return home, eventually."

Roland sat up straighter. "Is it really possible to leave this place? I've tried, but—" He hesitated.

"I know. It was surrounded by a ring of fear, but it was only caused by vVos devices. I, and some friends, found a way to disarm the devices. The way is now clear to advance on the complex, but we must have as many as possible with us."

"I'll go," said Roland. "What sort of a future is there for me here? At least at home I knew who I was and something of those around me." He gave Leah an angry look, as if she had somehow betrayed him by not being what he had expected.

"It will be dangerous," she said, feeling she had to give him a last chance to back out.

"I think it's dangerous wherever we are," he said. "I'm not much one for premonitions, but ever since I arrived, I had the feeling that we were waiting for something to happen."

"We leave at first light," said Leah, not mentioning that she, too, had felt the pressure of time passing.

As she walked away, she was happy to have enlisted Roland's help, but she couldn't help regretting what they had lost. *I'll be glad when this is all over and he's back in his own world, and I in mine.* She didn't want to admit that they had come from the same general time period, and in effect the same world.

As sunlight edged the rugged mountain range with flame, Leah and Scorpio, followed by their "army," walked past what had once been the fear-barrier, but was now only a row of trees. Leah looked back at the motley assemblage. Vikings, knight, samurai, frontiersman, African huntress, Egyptian, female aviator, Aborigines, and more—a strange cross-section from Earth's history. They still could barely understand each other and would be aghast at some of their companions' beliefs and customs.

"Do you think we have a chance against the vVos?" asked Scorpio.

"We really don't know what we're fighting," said Leah, "but we have to try."

"I don't know," said Scorpio. "The labs weren't exactly a fortress, but there were lots of the vVos there." He looked up and saw a familiar shape in the sky. Climbing to the top of a rock he began to wave his arms wildly. Leah thought he had lost his mind until a large winged creature began to soar nearer.

Finally it swooped down and landed.

"Fz!"

"Scorpio! I waited," said Fz, pointing to himself to make himself clear.

He was about to continue to pantomime, when Scorpio said clearly in the language of the wefft, "I was in there a long time. I couldn't expect you to wait forever."

Fz looked surprised at this magic, but accepted it.

"What is . . . this?" The wefft gestured toward Leah and Scorpio's army, now settled in to eat a makeshift meal. They had overthrown the vVos waiters and gathered up as much food as they could carry.

Scorpio explained what had happened.

"Marching on that place sounds dangerous," said Fz. "Maybe I'd better go with you, as a scout."

"We'll be glad of your help," said Leah.

The vVos unit that Scorpio had crushed continued to creep untiringly. It took it a very long time, but it crossed the mountains and approached the fear-barrier of the Human Compound. Of course the barrier, designed to affect human minds, had no effect on it. It entered the compound, passing through the White Grove, now deserted except for a few units in sloth bodies that continued to walk about with trays, though there was now no one to serve. When their term of service was up, they would abandon the bodies and return to the cluster, but until that time, they kept on following orders.

The unit looked about hopefully, but all these bodies were occupied. It continued on its way. Occasionally in its travels it passed a small animal and veered in that direction, but the animals were too lively to be caught by the unit in its present condition. At last it blundered between some rocks and into a cave. It was about to retrace its steps when it saw a body, lying at the back of the cave. Someone had covered its face with a small cloth; that was the extent of the funeral amenities.

The unit went over to the body and touched it with its antennae. It didn't try to move away. Under normal circumstances a vVos would not think of inhabiting a dead body because of the aesthetics of the thing. They battened on the emotions of the living. However, these circumstances weren't normal. The damaged unit had little chance of catching up with a living organism and it had been directed to possess a body. In its befuddled state, Cnozca's body seemed fair game.

There was already an opening at the back of the neck, so that part went quite well, but when it began to insert its filaments, it realized that something was wrong with this body. The brain was almost devoid of emotion; only a faint residue lingered. When the unit tried to make it rise, it moved like a robot. It was difficult to make it move on muscles that had stiffened. Still, the the vVos had accomplished its mission, to possess a body. Now the second directive kicked in: Return to the cluster. Riding this body would not be pleasant, but the vVos could make it move. He would follow the second directive.

Someone had sealed the body in, using heavy rocks, but the vVos set Cnozca's muscular shoulder to pushing them aside, and after some hard work, the body could emerge from the cave. It would have made a frightening appearance if anyone was there to see it: a stiff-muscled figure with discolored skin and a face warped out of all semblance of anything human. The vVos walked the body toward the fear-barrier. As Cnozca crossed the zone where the vVos's devices were still broadcasting their message of fear, the powerful broadcast began to work on his brain. Since the unit was damaged, its control was not perfect. As Cnozca's brain was brought to life again, the unit felt its control slip. Now the unit was a passenger in the body.

The withered lips writhed. "Heart," the thing said in a croaking voice. Cnozca had been buried with his only remaining pieces of property, his cloak and the obsidian dagger. Now a gnarled hand closed on the dagger. "Heart," the lips repeated, and Cnozca strode out of the Human Compound with yet a third directive fixed in his muddled brain.

Chapter Sixteen

Scorpio and Leah's army separated as they came to the forest surrounding the laboratories and used the cover to move up closer. Fz came swooping through the trees and landed beside Scorpio. "There is little activity outside the buildings."

"They disseminate information quickly," said Scorpio. "I don't know how. Perhaps they are waiting to trap us."

"We'll have to take that chance," said Leah, and with a wave of her arm sent her troops into battle. The humans rushed toward the buildings, weapons held at the ready. Leah and Scorpio joined them, waiting for the first burst of laser fire or the sound of a bomb. The leaders reached the large doors and, oddly, found them open.

"All right, we'll go in," said Leah. "But be on the alert." The invaders ran through the corridors, dashing into different rooms, shouting war cries or threats. Each room was empty.

"Nobody is here," said Leah, chagrined.

A careful search of the labs told them that not only had all the scientists left, there were no written records, none at all.

"Search again," said Leah when she was told. "These are aliens; perhaps the records are in a form you did not recognize. Look everywhere. A civilization depends on its ability to keep records, since individuals can't remember everything."

A second search turned up nothing.

"We're beaten," said Leah. "Time is running out, and we still know nothing about our purpose here, or what's going to happen. They didn't have to fight to defeat us."

"Look, I've taken a prisoner." Scorpio and Leah looked up and saw Fz hopping toward them. He trailed a wefft-woven cord and its other end was tied about the neck of a hairy vVos creature.

"Perhaps we can question him," said Scorpio.

Leah moved toward the the vVos as menacingly as she was able. "You will tell us everything," she said. "Or you'll wish you'd never been born."

The vVos creature shuffled its large furry feet. A low whistling call came from its invisible mouth.

"Talk," said Scorpio, "and be quick about it, or—"

As they watched in amazement, the creature sat down on the floor and began to rummage in its long fur. A moment later it pulled out a fat insect that it cracked in its teeth before eating.

"This is an animal," said Leah in disgust.

"Perhaps it's only pretending, so that we won't hurt it," said Scorpio, inspecting the creature more carefully.

The sloth sat there rocking back and forth on its buttocks, occasionally picking up one of its feet to inspect the sole.

"No, look at it. Do you think such a thing could be intelligent, could learn the Aquay tongue, could build spaceships? Is this a vVos or isn't it?"

Scorpio and Leah looked at each other and it was as if their thought were a spark jumping the gap between them. "What if—" said Leah. "What if this was only a vVos's body, or a body it could use. Or is that idea totally crazy? Could this just be a distant cousin of the intelligent vVos?"

"So if it could use the body of this hairy beast, then why couldn't it use other bodies?" asked Fz. "Say the bodies of the wefft."

"Why would you ask that?" said Scorpio.

Fz told them about the fight he'd witnessed between the two wefft.

"Now it makes perfect sense," said Leah. "The fry and the men in the grove fought because their bodies were possessed. We've solved the puzzle."

"Then why don't you look happy?"

"We know what the vVos doesn't look like," she said, pointing to the hairy creature. "But we don't know what it does look like, and most importantly we don't know where to locate them, and this is a big planet. Even if we began a search, it might be too late."

"So what do we do now?" asked Scorpio.

"I'm not sure," said Leah. She looked around at the other humans. "I suppose everyone could use a rest, so we may camp here for a while. At least we have shelter. Maybe we can figure out a plan of action."

"What should I do with this hairy one?" asked Fz.

"Let it go," said Scorpio, "unless you want to keep it as a pet."

"I've already got a pet," said Fz, and he and Scorpio laughed.

The Cnozca body reached the foothills and began to climb. It was easy to see that a large group of people had passed this way. They had crushed down grass and foliage and left debris from their meals. He remembered particularly a thin, brown girl. That was the time he had come the closest to realizing his dream. If she was with these people, perhaps he could find her again.

The sun had not been kind to his several-days-dead body. When he struggled to climb up a narrow trail, bits of skin and flesh were left behind on the rocks. Both the unit and what remnant was left of Cnozca's consciousness were aware that time in this body was limited. Beneath Cnozca's need for a sacrifice, the unit still felt its desire to return to the cluster, but for once the vVos was only a passenger in a body. The vVos could only bide its time.

Leah sat outside the lab, enjoying what was left of the afternoon. Eric and Jed were playing a game that involved trying to stick their knives into a circle drawn on the ground. Jed had initiated it and since his bowie knife was exquisitely balanced he was winning most of the time. Eric's knife was only a shard of bronze with leather wrapped around the tang to form a handle. Still, watching them play the game, substituting gestures for words when necessary, gave her a feeling of hope. Humans could learn to live together and cooperate even without a common language and common social mores.

She looked up into the sky and saw that the hazy pink puffballs of cloud that usually formed at sunset had been replaced by a wall of thunderheads dyed bloodred by the setting sun. The wind had picked up, too, raising the dust, and lightning played on the flanks of the clouds.

"Might get a storm tonight," Jed called over his shoulder to her. "My bunion is sayin' 'howdy.' "

Bone Man with Chumyip at his shoulder appeared before Leah and stood like pillars of ebony in the fading light. They didn't approach like ordinary humans, they were always just "there." They weren't so much stealthy as unobtrusive, she decided. She had seen them waiting outside a small animal's burrow with patience more than human. Eventually the animal would emerge and fall prey to their weapons.

The two Aborigines stood waiting for her to speak.

"Is there a problem?" she asked. "I thought you were on watch."

"Bone Man says a bad thing comin'," said Chumyip, who usually did the talking for the old man. Bone Man must be too mystical to indulge in mere speech, Leah decided, then thought. No, everything they do has a reason. It's just that I never know what it is.

"If something is coming, then why did you abandon your post," said Leah, wondering if standing watch might not be a little too much for the Aborigines.

"Long way off," said Chumyip. "Miles away."

"If your 'bad thing' is so far away, then how do you even know it's coming?"

"Smell him," said Bone Man, speaking for himself this time, a grin making his dark skin spread into thousands of wrinkles.

"Well, go back to your duty. You'll be relieved in due time." Bone Man looked up at the sky. "If a storm comes, we'll stand watch by the main doors."

Bone Man saluted with his spear as he left.

Smell him coming indeed, thought Leah. "I can see I'm going to have my hands full with this crew."

She heard shouting and turned to see Eric and Jed grappling and rolling on the ground, each trying to choke the other. She heard Eric rasp, "Spit on me, curse me, will you, I'll send you to meet your ancestors, whatever they were."

"I'm a ring-tailed, side-winding catamount from hell and I'm gonna have your gizzard, you—" shouted Jed in return.

Leah decided that Jed's disgusting habit of chewing leaves to a pulp and spitting them had clashed with the earlier man's taboo against bodily fluids. Leah picked up a long metal pipe that some fleeing vVos worker had left in the grass and brought it down on the two combatants hard enough to get their attention.

"Listen to me," she shouted, alternating between Jed's language and Eric's. "I'm the only one here who can get you home again. Unless you want to lose that chance, I suggest you mind your manners!"

They sat up, looking at her embarrassedly and brushing the dirt off their clothes. They went inside in a surly manner, but left each other alone.

Leah was surprised the brawl had been settled so easily. Sometimes she had to call in Scorpio and Roland to back her up. It was inevitable that differing backgrounds led to conflicts. Maybe if they were here for a long time, this group would meld into a society, keeping the good parts of what they had brought from Earth and dropping the bad. It was a nice dream.

All I have to hold over their heads is the promise of returning home. They all want that. So I'd better try my best to get this resolved so there's someone left to go home.

When the wind began to come in gusts and the sound of thunder rolled across the sky, Leah called in the watch and posted them by the doors of the building the humans had converted into their camp.

The structure was flimsily built and Leah could feel the walls vibrate as the winds struck them.

"The vVos didn't build for the long-term," said Scorpio, helping her to secure one of the narrow windows against the shrieking wind.

"If one must build, why not build for the ages," said Hatshepsut, who was standing nearby and overheard them. Scorpio had spoken in Aquay but she was learning it.

"They may be aware that all buildings and monuments crumble, eventually," said Leah.

"Pyramids do not crumble," said Hatshepsut and turned and walked away.

"Feeling a little down tonight?" Scorpio asked Leah.

"I'm in a strange mood," she said. "I guess it's the storm. Two different members of the watch have reported seeing a figure creeping around the grounds. One of them thought he was trying to look through the window. I can't be sure they really saw anything. When the vVos collected primitive people, they collected a whole orb load of crazy superstitions. Hatshepsut keeps looking over her shoulder as if she might see a dead man coming after her. The Vikings saw me using the orb and they're convinced I'm a Valkyrie."

"One being's crazy superstition is another's religion," said Scorpio. "But we should keep our eyes open. We don't know enough about the vVos to know what they're capable of."

Taking the full brunt of the storm, Cnozca paced about the grounds, rain washing over his skin, plastering down his hair and garments until he looked like an ambulatory statue of bronze. From a distance he could see that the doorways were guarded. As he stalked stiffly along, he stumbled over something. Reaching down, he discovered it was a sort of trapdoor. His fingers no longer worked well, but he managed to get the trapdoor open. There were metal steps going down into a basement below the building. He descended, finding a complex of large air-ducts that branched throughout the labs. He crawled along one, leaving a lot of his skin behind, though he didn't feel it.

From these, he could peer into various rooms that housed the humans, searching for the particular one he had chosen.

• • •

After the great storm had passed, Hatshepsut settled onto her makeshift bed and wrapped a blanket around herself.

This was the second night in the makeshift camp the humans had established. The first night she had been exhausted after the long trek and the excitement of taking the lab complex. Leah had said that when the humans were safe from the vVos, something Leah called an orb would return and they would all be able to go back to their own times. Though Hatshepsut didn't want to return to the exact moment she was carried off, returning to her comfortable life at court was a tempting thought.

However, she now felt different about at least some of the humans now sharing the same room. She didn't have to lift her head to see several blanket-wrapped forms nearby. At first the others who had shared her captivity were frightening because of their babbling voices. The march had given them the beginnings of understanding, since they had had to cooperate, and a simple language of hand gestures was beginning to evolve. The faces were no longer so unfamiliar, even though they were still strange.

She listened to the night noises, the far-off cries of alien animals and birds, the creaking and settling of the building and the wind swooping around the walls. Finally they lulled her to sleep.

Though she had fallen asleep with good thoughts in mind, her dreams soon became troubled. She saw a tall shape looming over her, the intent clear, as a black knife blade descended to slash and tear her flesh. Hands reached deep into the wound in her chest, bringing out a dripping dark lump that pulsed, pulsed.

Hatshepsut awoke with a suppressed scream. She sat up, looking around wildly, unsure of where she was at first. She waited for her heartbeat to return to normal. The other sleepers in the room didn't stir. *An evil dream*, she thought. *I wonder if the burial we gave the madman was honorable enough. Perhaps his* ka *is not appeased.*

She heard footsteps in the corridor outside.

She supposed it was only someone retiring late, but as she listened she realized there was something wrong with the sound of the footsteps. The cadence was slowed as if each step were an effort, then she heard the sounds no more. She forced herself to turn over and try to go back to sleep. Because there were few windows, the room was stuffy and Hatshepsut began to smell an oppressive odor, as of meat gone bad.

She threw back the blanket. It was no use. She wasn't going to get any sleep this way. Too late she realized that someone had crept across the darkened floor on hands and knees as her own blankets were thrown back over her head and unyielding arms went around her body. Her scream was muffled in the blanket and she felt herself picked up and carried on unsteady feet. The rotten smell was so close she was choking on it.

Frozen with fear, Hatshepsut felt herself pulled into a round, narrow opening and then dragged along. After a time, they reached the end of this passage and then she was carried again. At last Hatshepsut felt cool air touch her bare legs and realized she was outside.

Too long I've been the obedient daughter, she thought. *Perhaps the god who granted my wish of wanting to make my own destiny wanted to teach me something*. Hatshepsut began to kick and struggle. Whoever had captured her was strong, but there was something wrong with his reflexes. As she gave a convulsive kick, she fell free and dropped to the ground, the blanket falling away from her face.

Hatshepsut screamed when she saw what had carried her from the room. It didn't move like a human being anymore, but like some out-of-control machine. Hatshepsut tried to scramble away, but it grabbed her again, pushed her down, raised the knife over its head.

Chapter Seventeen

The report of a revolver made it hesitate, look around. The first bullet went over the thing's head, but the second hit it squarely in the chest. It jerked reflexively, but recovered and began to come after Hatshepsut again.

Hatshepsut heard human voices and cried out for help. Several figures were running toward her. She recognized Scorpio, who stepped between Hatshepsut and Cnozca, moving in close to hammer at Cnozca with a barrage of quick blows. When Cnozca did not stagger backward, Scorpio looked surprised. Then Cnozca went on the attack, sweeping his knife in an arc. Scorpio cried out and grasped his side. Blood quickly seeped out between his fingers.

"Heart," said Cnozca in a bubbling voice, advancing on the wounded Aquay.

By this time Roland and several others had arrived. The knight ran forward, swinging something over his head. The spiked ball of the mace made contact with the Cnozca-thing's head with a sickening crunch. Surprisingly, after such a wound, it didn't fall, but it stood still, teetering a little. Suddenly, as if a decision had been made, it turned and began to run through the trees. Roland gave chase, swinging the mace over his head, as if eager to end the fight.

Hatshepsut was shaking with sobs and barely recognized Leah.

"It was the *ka* of the madman we buried," said Hatshepsut.

"Hush, it was no such thing. I told you that the dead don't walk," said Leah.

Scorpio walked slowly toward them. "I'm afraid she may be right," he said. "I saw the thing's face. It had changed a lot, but it did resemble the man we buried." He still held his hands tightly over his side. Leah drew them back so she could see how bad he was wounded.

A deep gash crossed his ribs. She tore a piece off the bottom of her T-shirt to use as a bandage. "You're badly hurt," she said. "Maybe you were hallucinating."

Roland returned, saying, "I gave chase but lost him in the darkness. I can't believe he ran off after the blow I gave him. His skull must have been crushed."

"I still say that the dead don't walk," said Leah. "And since they don't, something else impels it."

"The vVos," said Scorpio.

Leah jumped to her feet. "Everyone, search the woods! We must find that corpse. When we do, we'll follow it."

• • •

The Cnozca-body walked purposefully among the trees, its head at a skewed angle. The blow from Roland's mace had shattered the skull, driven out the last vestiges of Cnozca's consciousness and restored control to the unit. "Home" was the sole directive, as the damaged unit yearned to merge with the cluster.

Leah supported Scorpio and led him back to the lab. Hatshepsut followed, keeping close to them. "We'll get someone to do a better job of dressing that wound," she said.

"I'm sure it's not so bad," said Scorpio, though he walked stiffly as if he was in pain. "I'll still be able to help you if you locate the vVos's hiding place."

"I'm afraid you'll have to stay behind," said Leah.

"What's happened?" asked Fz as they returned to the lab.

"Scorpio has been wounded," said Leah. "Can you care for him, and if necessary keep him here by force if we have to leave?"

"I'd be glad to," said Fz, making sympathetic clucking noises as he examined Scorpio's wound.

Ito the Samurai hurried in. "We located the, er, thing you're looking for. We didn't try to stop it, but Jed is keeping it in sight."

"Good," said Leah. "I'll get everyone together. We'll leave at once."

Flying spies returned to the cluster. There was an even greater activity as the vVos mobilized itself in its own defense.

A possessed human body is about to lead the escaped humans to our cluster. How could such a thing happen? We don't know. There are always problems when dealing with unknown species. Remember the Ronicci? Who could forget. It was a disaster. The human body has been dead for some time. Do the dead of these humans walk as a general rule? I don't think so, and unless there was a unit involved, it would not know the way to the cluster. What can we do? There's only one thing we can do and that's to begin the Games. But the Games are several days away. The Games have never been held early. It is unheard of. But it is still necessary. Will we have the time for all of our number to extrude wings and legs before the humans reach us? No, but we can gain the time we need by sending out some advance scouts to possess the black lizards and bring them back here to defend our cluster. Yes, that's a good idea. When all is ready, we'll swarm out and begin the Games.

From a distance Leah watched the small figure of what had once been Cnozca toiling across the barren landscape. The forest had gradually given way to desert. Bushes like grotesque sculptures of barbed wire were the only plants. The head of the thing lolled to one side or the other, the legs were unsteady and it followed an erratic course.

The process of dissolution was making the body hard to control. Leah could only hope that it held together long enough to lead them to the vVos's hiding place. The feeling she had about time running out was very strong now.

After several more hours, the corpse staggered, the legs buckled and it went down. It got back onto hands and knees and began to crawl. It started to inch its way up a bald-topped hill where the constant wind made dust devils dance.

Someone at the back shouted above the whine of the wind. "Leah, look!" As Leah turned, she saw a formation of black shapes in the sky. They flew in a loose V shape, and her first guess was that they were birds. However, as they came closer, she saw that they were much larger than that.

"The dragons!" She recognized Roland's voice and saw that the oncoming beasts might resemble dragons a little: two pairs of transparent wings with a slithery body in the middle.

The lizards flew over the heads of the humans, the hum of their wings deafening, and then landed, forming a rough semicircle about the bald-topped hill.

The corpse was barely moving now, but still it inched forward. It had reached the top of the hill and now it stopped. None of the humans saw the damaged unit crawl free of the body and enter the entrance to the cluster, but they did see Cnozca's battered body give up its last form of life and sprawl in the dust with what looked like a great shudder of release.

"Their hideout has to be atop that hill!" shouted Jed. "Else why the flying lizards?"

"I think you're right," said Leah. "And we have to break through that defense." She signaled her army to advance.

Scorpio tossed about on the pallet that Fz had prepared for him, so much so that the wefft came over. "Are you feverish?" asked the anxious creature, touching Scorpio's face with long fingers.

"I'm only restless," said Scorpio. "I know I was too weak to go with Leah and the others, but I'm too strong to wait here patiently."

"I'm afraid that's all you can do," said Fz.

Scorpio rolled over and closed his eyes. It was so difficult to be here when Leah and the rest faced such a challenge! It was also next to impossible to sleep with that golden gleam in the room. He needed to ask Fz to cover the window. As he opened his eyes, he saw the orb, much enlarged, lying a few yards beyond him. *Now I don't have to be left behind,* he thought. Before he crawled toward the orb, he spared a glance over his shoulder to see what Fz was doing. The wefft might not think he was fit for orb travel. Fz was drowsing at the bedside, his eyes hooded.

Carefully Scorpio eased himself off the pallet and grasped the orb. Fever from the wound had muddled his thought processes. Though the orb was a powerful healing device, his first coherent thought was, *I must go and help the others.* He willed the orb to jump to wherever Leah was. The orb bubble formed around him, but again, the orb was not so obedient as it had once been. He found himself in orb space receiving visions.

The first was a montage of cataclysms. Beings of all sorts engaged in war. Whole cities exploded as their inhabitants scattered. Other scenes showed famines. Mothers holding starving babies. Fathers locked in combat over a small morsel of food. Scenes of pestilence were also included. Mass open graves waited for wagons loaded with bodies. The dead lay in the streets, unburied.

Enough! screamed Scorpio. *What has all this to do with me?* The scenes continued without letup, agonizingly graphic, and then by slow stages he began to realize that these were scenes of the future in this universe. In some way the presence of the alien orbs and the constant moving through time and disturbing the natural flow of things would eventually tilt the future toward events of catastrophe and chaos. He began to have the idea that the continued presence of the orbs and continued use of them would eventually destroy this universe altogether.

But I'm only one being, thought Scorpio. There's nothing I can do.

New pictures burst upon his already overloaded senses. As he watched, he saw a barren hilltop and then a horde of marching figures. It was the humans. *Yes, that's where I wanted to go*, he thought.

And then the scene changed. There was a gloom that suggested darkness, though he could still see pretty well. The light had an amber tinge, and by this he could see a great jellylike mass. It did nothing except quiver occasionally throughout its great bulk, as if some perturbation worked its way through it, as if some change were about to occur.

Along the edges of the thing, sections began to break loose. Long insectile legs began to poke from the shapeless mass and wings began to sprout. Scorpio was shocked when he saw their azure edges and remembered the confrontation with the alien insect. If he had had a neck in orb space, it would have tickled with the feeling of insect legs walking about on it. More and more sections of the great cluster broke apart until there were thousands of units, each transforming itself into a mothlike creature. When there reached a critical mass of insects flitting about inside the burrow, they began to shoot from the opening above until a massive cloud was formed.

Leah, watch out! Scorpio warned. *Now I know how the the vVos possess people.* The insects scattered on the wind. After a time, Scorpio saw the humans begin to fight among themselves. He knew they wouldn't stop until all, or almost all, were dead. His anxiety lessened as he realized this was still only an orb dream. He was being shown what could happen, not what would or had happened. So he supposed there was something the orb wanted from him, and he waited.

The scene was again the nightmare burrow with its huge quivering mass of creatures. The vVos were not the only inhabitants however. The amber light he had noticed earlier came from a small orb resting alongside the cluster.

The last, Scorpio thought, echoing what the orb was telling him. They put the last orb in here for safekeeping. All the other orbs have combined. If I can somehow get this orb into the burrow to combine with the other one, we will be saved. He wasn't sure how this would come about, but he was now certain of it. Then take me to the hilltop, he ordered.

Chapter Eighteen

When the orb bubble burst, Scorpio found himself back in the laboratory. Fz awoke from his doze with a surprised look. For *some reason I can't use the orb as a craft,* Scorpio thought.

"Fz, remember when we first met and couldn't even understand each other. Somehow we became friends anyway, without language. I must ask you to do something for me, and you must not question. You must simply do it as my friend."

Fz studied Scorpio for a moment. Scorpio struggled to keep his movements steady, his voice calm. If Fz thought he was only delirious and hallucinating, he might well keep him prisoner here while vVos overcame the humans.

Fz was silent a moment. "All right," he said.

Roland felt Noir's body tremble as the wind blew the alien scent of the black dragons to the horse's keen nostrils. Roland saw Leah's signal to attack and hesitated. When she had promised some hope of leaving this accursed place, he couldn't stop himself from following her. A woman as commander didn't seem so ridiculous in this place as it might have in his own world, and for some reason Leah was the only one who could communicate efficiently with everyone. She was probably the only one who could have created an army of such disparate folk.

From his viewpoint the march had accomplished little. They had attacked a fortress with no defenders. They had driven off an animated corpse. He marveled at how easily he accepted the impossible these days. Now they were being asked to break through a line of fearsome beasts to capture a barren hilltop, for no purpose he could see. Memories of minstrel tales of wandering knights on quests who overcame strange beasts and rescued fair damsels came to him, but he had always listened to these with a fair amount of amusement.

In his experience, being a knight had little to do with quests and magics. Warfare was swift and bloody. Powerful families fell and lands changed hands. Now that he found himself confronted with a score of real-life dragons, he wasn't so sure he was up to the challenge.

The black dragons were immense, with jagged teeth in their mouths, even though he didn't think they breathed fire. As he rode Noir at a walk, in order not to outstrip the rest who were on foot, he began to have second thoughts about the march and about Leah's leadership. She was only a woman and of a hated people. Why should he risk his life in such an ambiguous cause?

Gradually as the army moved up, he reined Noir farther to the side. As the forerunners launched an attack and the dragons flew to meet it, Roland reined Noir in and turned him. When the battle was met, dragons descended on the humans, snapping with immense jaws and using their tails to send people flying. Roland saw Eric slash at the scaly hide until the jaws caught him. He was shaken as a dog shakes a rat and thrown aside. He saw N'yuku throw her spear and transfix a lizard's thin body. All of the humans, including the small

Hatshepsut, were whaling away at the attacking lizards with whatever weapons they had.

Roland felt a sudden intense shame. He wheeled Noir about and spurred him into the fray. He whirled his mace about his head and brought it down on the shoulder of a dragon. The joint shattered; the delicate wing was torn to tatters. As it fell helplessly to earth, writhing, he moved in on it. Noir must have seen some movement because he leapt sideways just as the lizard's tail slashed past. Moving in again, Roland brought the mace down on the lizard's head. The body didn't stop squirming or the tail lashing, but it was otherwise dead. *They can be killed,* he thought. *They are only black lizard creatures, not dragons.*

As the fighting continued, Roland saw Leah keeping a dragon at bay with blows of the long metal pipe she had appropriated from the laboratory. As she tried to strike it again, it took the pipe in its jaws and tore it out of her grasp. She turned to run, but the lizard pounced, knocking her to the ground.

It was reaching down to catch her in its jaws when Roland rode up, aiming a blow at the vulnerable wings. The tail swung back quickly, knocking Noir off his feet and sending Roland crashing to the ground. Quickly the lizard turned its attention to Roland, leaping for him with jaws open, faceted eyes glittering.

Roland's mace had bounced out of his reach. The sword was still hanging from his saddle. He was unarmed and helpless. His eye fell upon the black bracelet that Leah had given him, years ago, it seemed.

"Touch this button and renew our love," she had said. A foolish conceit and yet it still meant something to him. With jaws hurtling toward him, his last action might as well affirm the love he still felt, despite his attempts to crush it. His finger touched the firing stud and a last bit of residual energy sizzled out, catching the lizard in the face.

It wasn't a powerful bolt, just a jet of energy, and yet the red flare bursting in the lizard's face was enough of a surprise that it stopped in its headlong charge long enough for Roland to scramble forward and grasp the mace. As it leapt forward again, he struck at an eye, crushing the delicate facets. As it backed away in pain, he struck again, blinding it. It blundered away helplessly.

Roland was glad to see that Leah was sitting up. She held her hand to the side of her head and a little blood was leaking down her cheek.

"Did you see?" he asked, coming over to her. "Your token must have had magic in it." He lifted her gently to her feet and put his arms around her.

"Only a little," said Leah. "Only enough."

Inside the burrow in the orb's pale light, the creatures along the edge of the cluster began to separate and to grow wings and legs. The Games! The Great Games are at hand! percolated through the mass of brain matter. Our lizards are holding the humans at bay. Soon the recalcitrant humans will fight in earnest to the glory of the vVos! And we will drink deep of their deaths to quench our thirst.

Fz saw the battle before Scorpio did. "There they are!" he shouted back into the wind. Scorpio held on tenaciously, realizing that everyone else had been right about his wound. It had weakened him more than he had thought. His greatest fear was losing consciousness and falling off. He didn't dare tell Fz that he was feeling weak, because the wefft would most certainly turn back.

He peered down at small figures like toys. Lizards in the air swooped on humans; those on the ground leapt and snapped fiercely. He saw human bodies scattered about and a few dead lizards, too. He didn't dare let himself think of Leah or to try to activate the telepathic contact they could sometimes achieve. He would have been stopped cold if there was no answer on the other end. If she didn't make it through, he was still doing what she would have wanted.

Scorpio had hastily made a larger pouch to contain the orb and had tied it to his belt. Occasionally the orb sent him a picture of the vVos splintering off into individuals, but mostly it just radiated a bright, prismatic light through the thin cloth of the pouch.

As Fz flew overhead, two lizards detached themselves from the fighting below and rose, riding the wind. "You didn't say anything about there being black lizards in this," said Fz as if teasing, yet his voice held an edge of fear.

"We must outfly them, or outfight them," said Scorpio. "We must reach the opening at the top of that hill."

"I'll try," said Fz.

The first lizard closed quickly, its jaws gaping. Fz dodged and the jaws snapped on thin air. The tip of the swinging tail hit Scorpio. He scrambled madly to stay aboard. He felt the edges of the wound pull apart and the warmth of blood seeping out again. He wished for the warm pallet and a blanket that he could pull over his head to shut all this out.

Fz had hardly escaped the first lizard when the second was upon him. There was no choice except to grapple with it. They rolled in midair screaming and clawing at each other. Scorpio used both arms and legs and clung with the last of his strength, feeling the world turning upside down again and again.

When dizziness receded, he saw a lizard dwindling in size, rolling over and over as it fell, tatters of wing trailing behind it. "Fz, if we get through this, I'll see that the wefft know who saved them," shouted Scorpio. He saw that they were about to pass over the hilltop and took the orb from its pouch.

"Let's just concentrate on getting through it," Fz called back nervously.

As Scorpio turned his head, he noticed the second lizard was rapidly overtaking them again. Scorpio could see the strain of Fz's flight as he tried to go faster. He could hear the crackle of wing joints and saw the skin bellying in the wind like a taut sail. If they could only stay ahead a few more yards. If not, well, then nothing mattered. Scorpio poised to cast the orb, his strength gone, reality bannering around him like a curtain in a wind.

They passed over the hilltop scant feet ahead of the charging lizard. Scorpio threw the orb. It hit the ground bouncing and radiating rainbow light, and unerringly made for the opening to the cluster.

Something happened.

For a moment time stopped. The fleeing Fz with Scorpio on his back, the pursuing lizard, the humans below in whatever fighting stance they had taken, their enemies the lizards with mouths agape and bodies undulant. All stopped like statues for that fleeting moment.

The hilltop imploded. Rocks, bushes, sand and other debris were inhaled into the hole at a rapid rate. A sucking wind drew objects and people on the periphery toward the hill or toppled them. There was no sound when it happened, but when it was over, there was the look of a cataclysm. The hilltop had become a smoking crater. Foliage was flattened all around.

Scorpio extricated himself painfully from the thorn bush where he'd been thrown after Fz's awkward landing. He looked at the still fuming crater and knew that when the final two orbs combined, they had finally gained enough power to punch their way back into their home dimension, taking most of the vVos with them for the ride. *Survival of the vVos in the orbs' dimension was strictly the vVos's problem,* Scorpio thought. Still, he realized he hadn't been told that the orbs would be gone for a reason. He might not have cooperated if he'd known throwing the orb meant he would be now exiled to this world.

Fz was coming toward him, crest all awry, wearing a length of thorn creeper like a garland. The lizard nearby wasn't so lucky. It lay in an awkward posture, neck skewed to one side.

"At least we don't have to worry about him," said Fz.

"Yes we do," said Scorpio, limping over to where the lizard lay. Fz looked at him as if he were crazy as he waited. At last the skin on the lizard's neck opened up and a pair of wet gray wings emerged to wave in the wind. Scorpio waited until the insect had totally emerged, then swatted it with his hand.

"This is our enemy," he said, holding up his hand coated with gray dust and the insect's crushed body. "This is a vVos."

He climbed aboard Fz and had the wefft fly him back to where the humans and lizards had been fighting. For some reason the lizards weren't recovering as rapidly from the effect the orbs had caused, and the humans were eagerly accepting this advantage to kill them all.

He located Leah and told her about the insects, so she could instruct others to spread out over the battlefield and kill them as they emerged from dead lizards. With that Scorpio's voice faded as dizziness made him stagger and almost fall.

Roland caught him and lowered him gently to the ground.

Leah had to lean closer to hear Scorpio's words. "We don't want to leave enough of them to form a new cluster," said Scorpio. "I don't know if it's possible for them to reproduce."

"Rest now," cautioned Leah. "We'll take care of the rest."

"No, I have something else I must tell you," he continued.

He told Leah then what he had done with the orb and expected her to burst into tears.

She only took Roland's hand and smiled, Scorpio thought, rather foolishly.

"You don't understand. Without the orbs we're stuck here."

"That's not such a high price to pay, is it?" asked Leah. "Considering you saved the universe."

"Well, I don't know whether what the orbs showed me mirrored what will happen in the universe, or if they lied. Maybe they only wanted to go home."

"Can't blame them for that," said Roland, his expression equally fatuous in Scorpio's eyes, given the seriousness of the situation.

"Except that you don't always have to go home," said Leah. "Sometimes you just make a home where you are. There are a lot of good men and women here. The vVos were choosing for their own purposes, but they chose the strong, the active, the brave. We'll form a colony, create a new human society. You won't be left out, Scorpio. You have a whole new generation of Aquay to inspire."

"But I took you away from your own world, your own time, put you into terrible danger and stranded you here."

"I had already rejected my own time," said Leah, "and with the orb I couldn't seem to fit in anywhere. Without it I *must* learn to. Even if having the orbs didn't destroy the universe, they did destroy the will to work and learn. It was far too easy to jump out of one's troubles."

"But you'll never see Earth or Earth people again."

"Someday the people of Earth may visit us and marvel at the society we have created. Or if we grow too impatient for that to happen, there are always the vVos's well-stocked laboratories. A great deal could be learned from what they've already accomplished."

Scorpio looked at Roland and Leah, who were now hand in hand. "I can see that it suits you to stay here now, but what of them." He indicated the other humans. "You led them here with promises that they would go home."

Leah grew solemn. "I'll tell all of them that it's no longer possible to go home. Some may be unhappy and others will blame me, but I still did the best I could. As you did, Scorpio. Stop blaming yourself."

Hatshepsut approached them. "We've accounted for all the vVos in the lizards' bodies. We had to chase down a couple of them, but we got them all."

"Then the danger is past. Tonight we'll hold a celebration!" said Leah.

As the humans gathered to congratulate each other, a tiny form crept from the crater. Its body resembled a vVos insect, but it had no wings. Its abdomen was distended and elongated until it dragged in the dust. This was the Seeder, a specialized form that had not been needed for thousands upon thousands of years. It had lain dormant in a special chamber of the burrow until such time as its services were needed. Its abdomen was filled with thousands of tiny eggs that would create new vVos. All it needed to do was get under the ground where it could reseed the race.

The floor of the crater had fused into black glass from the force of the implosion, thus it couldn't dig straight down. It crept slowly over the lip of the crater and headed for a wide crack in the earth. Once it reached that opening it was safe.

Hatshepsut happened to be looking up at the crater when she noticed the insect toiling across the barren ground. "Is that one of them?" she asked, pointing at it.

Scorpio gathered his remaining strength and sat up, despite Leah's protest, looking in the direction Hatshepsut pointed. "That overlong body can only mean eggs," he said.

"We have to stop it." They were too far away to keep it from reaching that crack in the earth where it would no doubt burrow deeper. They heard the revolver's hammer click on an empty cylinder. All the ammunition had been used in battling the lizards.

"What can we do?" asked Leah, though it was obvious that no one could do anything. "Our troubles will begin all over again."

As she spoke a polished curve of wood sped upward toward the crawling insect. Some had seen it leave the hand of Chumyip, the Aborigine. The famous come-back boomerang was only a toy; the heavy artillery of the Aborigine was the throwing stick, and this one was thrown true. It smashed the insect into the ground before it could reach safety.

The humans began to cheer Chumyip. The words and phrases were different but they all meant the same thing. Bone Man beamed proudly. His mission begun so long ago was completed. His charge had become a man.

The End of Book 6

J. T. Colby & Company, Inc.
Purveyors of Time Travel Instruments and Accessories™

TIME TRAVEL ADVENTURES Published by iBooks:

THE "RAY BRADBURY PRESENTS" SERIES Dinosaur World
• Dinosaur Planet
Dinosaur Samurai • Dinosaur Warriors
Dinosaur Empire

TIME MACHINE™ SERIES

We welcome all feedback about the series.

Write or email to the editors at the following address:
J. T. Colby & Company, Inc.
Purveyors of Time Travel Instruments and Accessories™
Manhanset House Dering Harbor, New York 11965-0342
bricktower@aol.com • bricktowerpress.com

For sales, editorial information, subsidiary rights information
or a catalog, please write or phone or e-mail

IBOOKS
Manhanset House
Shelter Island Hts., New York 11965, US
Tel: 212-427-7139
www.ibooksinc.com
bricktower@aol.com
www.IngramContent.com

For sales in the UK and Europe please contact our distributor,
Gazelle Book Services
White Cross Mills
Lancaster, LA1 4XS, UK
Tel: (01524) 68765 Fax: (01524) 63232
email: jacky@gazellebooks.co.uk

www.ingramcontent.com/pod-product-compliance
Lightning Source LLC
LaVergne TN
LVHW010620100826
845148LV00014B/3041
* 9 7 8 1 5 9 6 8 7 6 7 3 6 *